COLD CRASH

ELLIE KLINE SERIES: BOOK THIRTEEN

MARY STONE

DONNA BERDEL

Copyright © 2024 by Mary Stone Publishing

All rights reserved.

No part of this book may be reproduced in any form or by any electronic or mechanical means, including information storage and retrieval systems, without written permission from the author, except for the use of brief quotations in a book review.

❦ Created with Vellum

This book is dedicated to the unsung heroes of philanthropy, those who give what they can, be it time, effort, or resources, to help others. Your contributions, big or small, create ripples of change and shine a light on the power of compassion.

DESCRIPTION

On a crash course with death.

Ellie Kline's return to the world of crime investigation is heralded by two unexpected texts. The first bears unsettling news from her mother...a family friend has been found dead under mysterious circumstances. Was it an accident, suicide, or foul play?

Before Ellie can process this family tragedy, the second text arrives, jolting her back into professional mode. The Charleston Police Department, grappling with a case that could shake the city's upper crust, lifts Ellie's suspension but pairs her with a partner to investigate the case.

A lone ranger at heart, Ellie isn't pleased.

But as a scion of a respected family, Ellie's deep roots in Charleston's elite circles make her the perfect choice to untangle the web surrounding one of their own's tragic end. Embarking on a journey through the labyrinth of high society, Ellie's search for the truth yields more questions than answers. Each interview leads to frustrating dead ends.

And more dead bodies.

With the line between ally and enemy blurring, Ellie's quest for the truth turns into a race against a killer determined to keep the past buried.

A killer's vendetta turns eerily personal in Cold Crash, the thirteenth book of Mary Stone's best-selling Ellie Kline series, thrusting Ellie into a deadly game where skeletons don't just lurk in closets—they lie in wait.

1

Monique LaPierre glided through the lavish gala, her senses tingling with a mix of excitement and unease. The room was a swirl of opulence, but beneath the surface, something felt amiss.

Or maybe it's just me.

She passed a cozy couple laughing near the cocktail bar. The woman, swaddled in a luxurious red satin gown with loose ruffles billowing to the ground, was part of the mayor's entourage. Her companion, sporting a black tuxedo with a silky bow tie almost the same shade as the woman's dress, was an actor. Just months ago, Monique had seen him battling aliens on a doomed cruise ship in the Bermuda Triangle, a far cry from the sophisticated world she was used to.

The movie's ridiculous premise was the complete opposite of the foreign and period films she and Hal used to watch, and she'd loved every minute. Sitting in the half-empty theater, munching on popcorn and laughing at the preposterous scenes until she cried, Monique had found freedom. An escape from the uptight, dulled glitz and glamour of her real life.

Since then, when her day-to-day responsibilities got too stifling, she closed her eyes and imagined the coolness of the dark theater and the taste of greasy butter on her lips. The memory calmed her anxiety during rough times.

Like tonight.

Perhaps I'll cancel my appointments tomorrow and catch the new Jennifer Aniston film instead. Just the thought of that minor rebellion brought a smile to her face.

Monique waltzed around a crowd of men—all dressed to the nines in pristine black tuxes and ties—and stepped toward a round table near the edge of the portico. She dropped into a chair and inhaled the mixture of bourbon, sweat, and cigar smoke swirling beneath the twinkling white lights above.

Exhaling, she massaged her aching shoulder. Political fundraisers exhausted Monique. Especially those meant to fund campaigns for politicians she didn't particularly care for, like tonight's big event for the mayor. Hal used to handle the schmoozing. All Monique had to do was show up, make nice chitchat, and look gorgeous.

But now her throat ached from talking so much, and her brain strained to remember all the names and positions of the people around her. The crescendo of voices from the dozens and dozens of rich attendees chattering around the room made her head ache.

I can't take much more socializing tonight.

She glanced at her daughter, who sat across the table with her eyes glued to her phone. At twenty-seven, Jackie appeared younger than her years in the pink halter frock she'd chosen. Her tawny shoulders glistened in the glow of the faux candles placed in a flower arrangement at the center of their table.

Monique frowned at Jackie's lack of investment in the party. Her daughter was too young to be so blasé about her status in society. *This is Hal's fault.* He'd spoiled her too much over the years, letting her skip events whenever she begged.

The LaPierre lifestyle came with responsibilities, which Monique assisted her husband in fulfilling for decades. Hal was gone now, and, at fifty-two, Monique had grown tired of the constant grind.

Soon, those responsibilities would fall on her daughter's unprepared shoulders. In the years since Hal's death, Monique had dedicated all her time and energy to preparing Jackie for a leadership role in society.

So far, she'd failed.

"*Meu anjo*, this will be your life someday." Monique brushed a thick, black curl off her neck. "Show a bit of interest in it, at least."

As Jackie's head shot up, her dangling diamond earrings flurried back and forth like tiny pendulums. She arched a perfectly plucked eyebrow. "My life? Uh-uh. No. I'd rather die than pander to these egotistical windbags."

A rush of heat singed Monique's cheeks. She swiveled her head, surveying the area for signs that anyone had heard her daughter's outburst. "Jackie! You can't—"

"This will never be my life. Clawing up the social ladder is your thing. Not mine." Jackie rose and grabbed her wine glass from the table, swallowing the rest of her drink in one gulp. She fluffed her own ebony strands and stormed off.

Monique's skin prickled as her daughter disappeared into the crowd. *Rotten child.* She immediately regretted the thought and sighed. Jackie wasn't rotten. A little spoiled and headstrong, but that was to be expected, considering they'd raised her with a silver spoon in her mouth.

A server appeared beside her with a tray of crystal flutes filled with champagne. "Madam?"

She reached for a glass before reconsidering and shaking her head. The server nodded and moved on. Feeling torn, Monique drummed her fingers on the white linen tablecloth. The mother in her begged her to chase after Jackie. The businesswoman in her advised her to get back to work. Both options would drain her energy.

Screw it. The wooden chair legs screeched when she stood. *I need fresh air and privacy.* She whirled and slipped through the crowd.

A man in a burgundy brocade jacket tugged at her elbow. "Monique! It's been ages. How have you been since…?"

His sentence trailed off in a way Monique had become well-accustomed to since her husband's death. She tilted her head and smiled. "Taking it day by day. Call me, and we'll get together for lunch, yes?"

Before he had time to answer, she stumbled toward the exit but was stopped again. This time, a woman in a white satin formfitting dress and huge blond bun approached her. "Oh, my goodness, Moni. I haven't seen you since Hal's funer…"

Bristling, Monique flashed a smile she hoped the woman didn't realize was fake. "You're right. Why don't we get together for a round of golf and catch up? Call me."

A man nibbling on a mini-tomato pie caught her eye, but she ignored him as she dodged between bodies, careful to avoid tripping on flimsy long skirts and shiny leather shoes. He left her mercifully alone as she cut through the crowd.

"Mrs. LaPierre?"

Her head jerked toward the familiar voice. *Dammit.* She and the development director of the local home health care agency had been playing phone tag for days. Shuffling away would be rude. Monique turned and feigned a chipper attitude. "Linda, I didn't know you were going to be here."

"I was hoping we'd run into each other. Been trying to touch base with you since Wednesday. You got a moment?"

Linda's shimmering blue dress hung loosely on her minuscule frame. The patent flats she wore raised her up an inch, at the most.

Sweat beaded on Monique's forehead. "Of course. What do you need?"

The noise, the bodies shoved together, all the commotion circling around her was too much. She had to escape.

"Nothing overly complicated. We need donations to build a new hospice house. I have specs and funding projections we could go over."

Monique's black strapless dress tightened around her chest, the damp fabric clinging to her body. She palmed at the jewels resting around her neck, desperately trying to ignore her increasing heart rate. The veins in her arms and legs pulsed angrily, and her lungs shriveled into dried-up sea sponges. Why was she still in this suffocating room?

"Yes, call the office first thing tomorrow morning. I'll have the receptionist put you through."

Monique waved at the other woman while she stepped away, jostling the eyeglasses on a man's face when she bumped into him to make her escape.

Two more friends caught her on her way to the door but released her after a round of gentle cheek pecks. By the time she pushed through the threshold and scurried along the black-and-white checkered floor of the Coastline Inn's elegant sunroom, her body cooled, and her heart palpitations slowed.

Relieved to find no one else inside, she took a deep breath. Grazing her fingertips along the white panels of the sunroom, Monique walked farther into the house.

The Coastline Inn, built in the late 1700s, was one of her favorite places in Charleston. She'd attended several events at the popular venue. Some were held in the glass-enclosed portico, like the mayor's political fundraiser. Others, like her cousin's wedding, took place on the magnificent lawn in front of the house's main entrance.

The river bordered the property on one side while gardens flanked by oak groves surrounded all the others. Her favorite aspect of the Coastline Inn, though, was how the home and its grounds transported her miles and miles away from the busy bustle of the city.

At the end of the hall, Monique spotted the base of the winding staircase. Chestnut-colored wooden steps and a curving line of creamy white balusters twined upward to the second and third floors, where guest suites waited for pooped partygoers to unwind.

The suites, added during one of the house's many renovations, oozed elegance. Detailed cornices hung above ornately printed carpeting draped over original wood floors. Mantels with intricate moldings showcased valuable ceramics and vases. Chandeliers lit the rooms, and majestic medallions adorned the doors.

Monique climbed the stairs as she drank in all the beauty and grandeur. With each step, the anxiety she'd harbored moments before drifted away. Once she reached the third-floor landing, her head and heart were clear.

To her right, a dimly lit hallway led to a row of guest suites. On the left, a wooden door with a stained glass window in its center waited at the end of the hall. Behind that door sat her favorite area of the Coastline Inn. Monique wandered down the lavishly decorated corridor toward that cherished space. As she passed, portraits of members of Charleston's elite from over the years gazed upon her.

A warm breeze rolled off the nearby river when she opened the door and stepped out onto the veranda. The structure, built with bluestone and concrete mixed with crushed oyster shells, wrapped around the entire house. Lush gardens and trees surrounded the property, but the view from that door was the best.

Monique stepped forward and rested her hands on the railing. Taking another deep breath, she relaxed her shoulders and let the rich, earthy scent of pluff mud and river water sink into her lungs. The breeze toyed with her curls. Beneath her, the water swirled in mad circles and bumped against large rocks placed between the house and the river's edge.

She leaned forward, squinting in the moonlight. Recent rains had flooded parts of Charleston, but she hadn't expected the sea level to still be so high. All the other times she'd stayed at the Coastline Inn, the water had been calm and serene.

As a strong gust of wind buffeted her, Monique shivered, instinctively gripping the railing for balance. She glanced down, a flicker of unease passing through her as she considered the perilous drop to the jagged rocks below.

Stepping back, she crossed her arms and marveled at the blanket of stars glittering in the night sky. This world was so beautiful.

Monique smiled, a grin of genuine happiness. *I'm so fortunate. More fortunate than the people I try to help.* Her face fell as guilt tugged at her heart. Maybe she'd visit Linda tomorrow, bright and early, instead of waiting for a phone call. She could make a real difference for the people at Linda's new hospice.

The floor behind her creaked. Monique turned and peered into the dim hall. Her momentary happiness soured as a shadowy figure approached. "Oh, it's you."

Another creak resounded, louder this time.

As a shiver of unease raced down her spine, Monique steadied her stance. She was a petite woman, but she could be intimidating when necessary. "What are you doing out here? Didn't you leave?"

The ominous sound of footsteps echoed, each step a defiant drumbeat in the quiet corridor.

Monique groaned. Was this some sort of intimidation tactic? She had been unequivocal earlier during their heated exchange. "I'm not going to change my mind. Nothing you say will make—"

In a blur of movement, powerful hands struck Monique's chest, sending her backward. She lost her breath as her spine crashed against the railing.

Gasping for air, she struggled to regain her footing, but another vicious strike left her reeling. Her heels slipped on the balcony's surface, the world tilting dangerously as she bent backward over the edge.

Monique's hands flailed, grasping in vain for something —*anything*—to grab onto. But salvation was out of reach.

With one last cruel shove, she flew over, toppling and spinning into the void. As she spiraled downward, her world moved in slow motion. The stars, the veranda, the moon, and the piazza blurred together, amplifying her terror.

The roar of the river grew louder, almost mocking in its fury. A strangled cry, raw and full of despair, lodged in her throat. Every instinct shouted at her to brace for the inevitable.

Before she could even begin to pray, the jagged rocks embraced her. The chilling finality of impact came mercifully swift—a bone-jarring collision that silenced everything.

2

The heels of Eleanor Kline's sandals slapped against tile as she strode into the Charleston Police Department. Two detectives sitting on the edges of their desks, holding coffee and chitchatting, glanced up and gawked at her. Another detective perusing a file while walking to his desk almost dropped the entire stack when she passed by.

She could almost read their minds. *Why is she back? Wasn't she suspended? How did she get out of trouble this time?*

Ellie ignored the surprised faces on her trek to Lead Detective Rachel Stoddard's office. A couple weeks had passed since her boss had called her in and suspended her. She cringed at the memory. Harsh words were tossed around, most of them by Ellie, and tempers flared. That meeting ended with her storming out of the Charleston Police Department.

Getting the call from Stoddard to work a case? No one was more shocked by the turn of events than her.

An hour ago, she'd been sitting in the school parking lot, waiting for her foster daughter, Bethany, to bounce out of the building after her classes so Ellie could surprise the little girl with a trip to the ice cream shop.

A text from her mom arrived first. A few distraught sentences with a link to an article. The body of her mother's friend, Monique LaPierre, was discovered on the rocks bordering the river below an elite celebration venue.

The call from Stoddard came next. Ellie gaped when the other woman told her that her suspension was being, well, suspended. Apparently, she wanted Ellie to assist with the LaPierre case.

Ellie gripped the strap of her bag as she approached Stoddard's office. The blinds were drawn. *Is that good or bad?* She shuffled to her boss's doorway and halted.

She didn't have to be here. During her suspension, Ellie thought long and hard about her options going forward, should the worst-case scenario happen—that being complete banishment from the Charleston PD. Right now, her stunned and grieving mother needed her more than the people of the city did.

The muscles in her neck tightened. Peeking past the doorway, she spotted Stoddard at her desk, hunched over her laptop. Ellie stepped back.

With time to reflect, she now understood why Stoddard and the Office of Internal Affairs had suspended her in the first place. Her actions in the Cupid Killer case had been unjustified. She'd tricked people into helping her get information, manipulated Stoddard's commands, and run off to a secluded house in the woods to catch the perp without telling anyone. Or even getting a warrant first.

She'd told herself that the end—saving the Cupid Killer's captive—would justify the means. Acknowledging the truth was a hard lesson.

Inside her bag, Ellie's phone buzzed. Probably her mother. *Make a choice. Are you going to walk in there and tell*

Stoddard you'll help, or are you going to say your afternoon's already booked and go spend time with your grieving mom?

Her last interaction with Stoddard earlier that morning had been civil enough. Stoddard even complimented Ellie on her actions in Long Field Township, where she, along with her family and her boyfriend, FBI Special Agent Clay Lockwood, had gone for a week's vacation.

Except Ellie had gotten very little relaxation. Dead bodies seemed to follow her everywhere, even when she chose to scoot away from Charleston for a holiday. She'd stumbled onto a crime scene the day after they arrived.

When Stoddard called her in after she and her family returned, Ellie hadn't known what to expect. She certainly hadn't believed Stoddard would pat her on the back for the way she handled herself in her pursuit of the Long Field Killer. Sure, they'd come closer to understanding each other in that discussion, but not enough for Ellie to let her guard down around the woman.

"Kline? That you?" Stoddard's voice echoed through the hall.

"Yes."

Ellie straightened her shoulders before stepping into the office. Not much had changed, except for a new motivational poster. *Teamwork, not me work.* The accompanying image conveyed a group of soldiers struggling to raise a concrete wall.

Stoddard waved at the hard-on-the-butt chairs in front of her desk. "Have a seat."

"I'd rather not." Ellie crossed her arms. "I need to get back to my mom. You called when I was picking Bethany up from school. I had to drop her off at Mom's, who's a wreck because she just found out her friend died. She needs me."

"So do we, Kline." Stoddard's tone was firm.

"Okay. I can help you out with this case," Ellie raised her

chin a little higher, "*if* you lift my suspension. Otherwise, I'm heading back to my mom's house to be a good daughter for a change."

Stoddard tilted her head and studied Ellie. Pursing her lips, she nodded. "I understand your dilemma. Let me fill you in on the case. You can decide what you want to do after."

Stoddard being reasonable? Ellie blinked. "Sure."

She walked to her boss's desk and dropped into a chair. Her bag sounded like it weighed twenty pounds as it *thunk*ed on the floor beside her.

"Our victim is Monique LaPierre. She's got friends in high places. One of those friends is the mayor's office, meaning we've got some additional pressure to make a quick collar in this one."

Ellie held up her palm. "Wait. So because the victim is rich and influential, we're going to cut through the administrative BS?"

Her mind drifted to Monroe Wieland and Omar Vincent, two victims in a previous case. They were considered gangbangers and riffraff. Ellie found her hands tied at every turn as she tried to find their killer because the department wanted to write the men's deaths off as gang violence. Regret stabbed her heart when she remembered that she'd had a chance to save Monroe.

For them, she would've gladly cut through the administrative red tape. Ellie crossed her legs and leaned forward. "If this is cutting the line for a political favor, count me out."

Stoddard shook her head. "It's not. It's just another case. One which, I have to admit, you are uniquely suited to investigate. Your family has money and connections. You move freely in this world. And…"

Ellie inched closer, practically hanging off the edge of her seat. "And what?"

Her boss sighed. "And you're one of my best homicide detectives. Even in the short time you've been gone, the difference has been clear. I need you on this one."

Oh, my...

Ellie grinned. "How much did it hurt to say that out loud?"

Stoddard smiled back before speaking through gritted teeth. "More than you know. Are you in or out?"

Ellie tapped her fingers on the armrest. If she took this case, she wouldn't be available to comfort her mom, but if she found Monique's killer, she could give her mom closure. "Okay. Catch me up on where we are."

"This is the workup on Monique LaPierre and the Coastline Inn." Stoddard pushed a manila folder across the desk. "The Coastline Inn is still an active crime scene. You might want to head over there before they wrap up for the day."

She opened a desk drawer and pulled out a familiar badge and gun. Excitement bubbled around Ellie's heart, and her fingers trembled when she slipped the badge and gun into her bag. She was back. Again.

"There's a lot riding on this for you, Kline." Stoddard settled back in her chair.

With a nod, Ellie rose. She reached down to grab her bag, clutching the folder to her chest.

"And Kline?" A tiny smirk played on Stoddard's face. "As part of your reinstatement, I've assigned you a partner. Detective Lancaster. He's already at the Coastline Inn."

A partner? Seriously?

Ellie bit her tongue. Letting Stoddard see her annoyance? Not a chance. Instead, she plastered on a smile and shrugged. "Fine with me."

Lancaster. Her mind scrambled to recall the other detective. Was he the one with the mustache? Or the glasses?

Her shoulders slumped. She couldn't jog an image of him into her brain.

A tiny, invisible hammer banged against her temple as she exited Stoddard's office and swept past the other detectives still gawking at her from their desks.

She waited until she was outside to huff and puff, where only birds were around to give her a glance.

A partner? Stoddard's amused expression streaked through her mind. She opened the door to her SUV and climbed into the driver's seat. Leaning against the headrest, she released a heavy sigh.

I've got to make this work. One way or another. But how?

Ellie twisted her key in the ignition, and the motor hummed to life. She sat still for a minute, allowing her mind to brainstorm ideas. None of the options she conjured satisfied her. With a grunt, she eased out of the parking lot and onto Lockwood Drive, still contemplating the question.

How am I going to do my job effectively with a babysitter breathing down my neck?

3

A lone vehicle sat in the visitor parking lot of the Coastline Inn when Ellie pulled up. She parked beside the other car, picked up her phone, and dialed her mother's number.

Her mom answered on the fifth ring. "Hello?"

"It's me. Are you doing okay?"

"I suppose." The hoarseness in her mother's voice was heartbreaking. "I just don't understand. Monique was a beautiful person. I mean, inside. A shining light in a sea of greedy politicians and shady social pariahs. She always fought for the goodness in people. I can't believe she's gone."

Ellie bit her lip. "I'm sorry, Mom." The words felt like a cop-out. An easy way to keep her mother's pain at arm's length.

From the other end of the line came a sniffle. "Well, having Bethany here is helping a lot. She's keeping me distracted. We're making paper dolls at the dining room table. Glitter is everywhere. She's such a happy little thing. Could she spend the night? I can drop her off at school tomorrow."

"Of course she can stay, but I'll swing by and pick her up

for school if you don't mind getting her ready. Give her a kiss for me, okay?"

Ellie debated whether to tell her mom about her new case. *Not now. It'll lead to questions I can't answer yet.* After making sure her mother was doing all right without her, she ended the call.

Her ankle, still a little sore from a stumble she'd taken while jogging during her trip to Long Field Township, cracked as she exited the SUV. She stuck her foot out and twirled her ankle in circles, releasing a few more cracks in the process. *Probably should get that looked at.* She gazed at the brick wall dividing the parking lot and the Coastline Inn.

She'd visited the exclusive venue once or twice before but had never been inside. In the center of the brick wall, a set of open wrought iron gates revealed the front of the property. Ellie followed the sidewalk to the front steps, passing a grand grouping of vibrant flowers enclosed by a circular bush on the way. Butterflies floated among the petals and blended in with the foliage.

Pushing through the heavy front door, Ellie stepped into an oversize foyer. Gilded wallpaper surrounded polished hardwood floors. Detailed moldings of nature fell over arched doorways. She glanced up at the enormous glass chandelier taking up most of the ceiling. Sunlight streamed in from a large window over the front door and reflected off the chandelier's crystals, sending little globs of light dancing along the walls.

The room was stunning.

"Detective Kline?"

When she turned, she spotted a man descending the curved staircase on the left. The lights bounced off his bald head, and sweat glistened on his dark skin like morning dew on a brown mushroom. Latex gloves stretched across his burly hands, and blue booties clung to his shoes.

Wendell Lancaster. Ellie finally remembered him. The year before, he'd solved a series of homicides around Cooper River. According to department gossip, he could be just as headstrong as her.

Ellie waved. "Yep. Detective Lancaster, I presume?"

The man continued down the stairs without answering. Behind him, an apple-shaped woman with a long, slender neck followed. With her thinning brown hair in a bun and her slim legs protruding from a mocha-colored dress suit, she resembled the ostrich Bethany had once fallen in love with at the zoo.

Ellie caught the shimmer of the woman's name tag in the light. She hurried to the base of the stairs. "Are you the inn manager?"

The woman nodded as her foot hit the last step. "Yes, my name's Taylor Hollback."

Lancaster crossed his arms. "You got any questions for her, shoot. I've already asked all of mine."

Ellie shifted toward the inn manager. "We'll need a full list of employees and guests that were here last night."

Taylor brushed a hand through her hair, trying to tame the frizzy flyaway hairs curling around her face in the heat. "Yes. I can gather that information for you."

Dampness formed beneath the bosom of Ellie's dress. Though the temperature outside was a bearable eighty-four, the foyer of the Coastline Inn was, Ellie guessed, a good ten or fifteen degrees higher. She fanned herself. "Is the AC off?"

"It conked out shortly after officers arrived. We have a repair person on the way, but he had a long list of folks to get to before us." Taylor tugged at her suit jacket like she wished she could rip the fabric off her body.

Ellie blew out a steady breath. "What about other people? Who was at the party besides employees and guests?"

"White Glove Catering Services. They're a third-party

catering company. They had waitstaff handling the food and passing out hors d'oeuvres." Taylor's flushed cheeks expanded as she exhaled, causing a loose tendril of hair to dance above her forehead.

"I'll need those names as well." Ellie scanned the walls, spotting one camera hidden beneath a cornice. "Do you have security cameras set up on the grounds?"

"You want the security footage? I've been reviewing it already. With him." The inn manager pointed at Lancaster.

The other detective nodded. "That's what I was doing upstairs just before you arrived. There's a problem. The third-floor cameras went out of commission at some point early in the evening yesterday. Can't see anyone coming or going."

"That's awfully convenient." Ellie chewed on a fingernail as she pondered other options. "Who was on duty last night? Security-wise?"

"Bernard Cookson." A disturbance clanked on the porch outside. Taylor rushed to open the front door. "Oh, thank god. Put one in every room."

A group of men trudged in carrying electric fans of varying sizes and models. One was plugged in near where Ellie and Lancaster stood. As fresh waves of cool air swirled around them, both detectives sighed in relief.

Lancaster leaned down toward Ellie's ear, his voice low. "You have no idea how hot it was upstairs in the security room. Like Hades in a heat wave."

Ellie chuckled. Perhaps having a partner wouldn't be so bad.

After Taylor finished instructing the men on what to do with the rest of the fans, she returned to Ellie and Lancaster. "Was there anything else?"

"That security footage." The video might be incomplete,

but Ellie still wanted to see it with her own eyes. "Can we get it on a thumb drive to take back to the station?"

"I'll talk to our IT guy about getting that taken care of right away." The woman scurried back up the stairs.

"Want to see the crime scene?" Lancaster gestured toward the stairs as well.

"I thought you'd never ask." Ellie reluctantly broke free from the buzzing fan's cool breeze and followed the other detective up the circular staircase. At the top, she accepted a pair of gloves and booties from the uniform monitoring the area.

Slipping beneath the crime scene tape draped across the entrance to the landing for the third floor, Ellie gawked at the exquisite ornaments and artwork on display. Thick rugs in vibrant colors ran down the hallway on each side. Paintings of Charleston's who's who, circa 1700 to 1900, dotted walls lined with an intricate spiraled flower pattern.

Ellie peered in both directions. A row of closed doors rested on one end of the hall. *Those must be the guest rooms.* On the other end stood a lone door with a stained glass window.

Lancaster walked to the door with the colorful glass and stepped outside, motioning for Ellie to join him on the balcony.

The river rushed beneath them, its swirling waters stirring up familiar scents of sour earth and fish that hit Ellie's nostrils the second she stepped outside. She meandered to the balcony's edge and glanced down. Yellow markers stuck out on the gray rocks to show where Monique's body had landed.

Her stomach clenched as she pictured her mother's friend lying across those rocks. Had she fallen over the rail by accident, or had someone pushed her? Or…had something been going on in Monique's life Ellie's mother didn't know about? Something so horrible that Monique had chosen to take her own life?

I'll find out.

The LaPierre family was well known throughout Charleston's social circles. Jackie LaPierre was close to Ellie's age. Growing up, they'd attended the same private school.

"A shining light in a sea of greedy politicians and shady social pariahs."

Ellie frowned. Her mother's assessment of Monique might have been right, but it didn't change the fact she was now dead...by her own hand or someone else's. Family friend or not, Ellie would have to expose the skeletons Monique LaPierre kept in her closet, and the idea of possibly tarnishing her mother's image of her friend gutted her.

Maybe I should've walked away from this case when Stoddard dangled it in front of me.

Lancaster cleared his throat. "Seen enough?"

Ellie sighed. "Up here? Yes. But I suggest we go speak with the front desk receptionist and take a closer look outside."

Her gaze drifted over the rocks below. A line of mud residue rose above the spot where the yellow markers sprouted. There'd been flooding in the past couple of days. Had the killer pushed Monique, thinking the river would wash away her body?

If so, the murder of Monique LaPierre wasn't a spur-of-the-moment decision. Ellie added the sudden lack of third-floor security footage into the equation. If this was a murder —and she was going to work the case as such until evidence told her otherwise—Ellie doubted the glitch was an accident. The killer had planned his or her moves with precision.

Had the well-respected Monique LaPierre died because she had a secret? If so, it was one Ellie intended to dig out of the LaPierre closet.

4

As Ellie proceeded to ask questions of the front desk receptionist, Lancaster stood a few feet away, taking down notes.

"I was here, sure." Clara Schuster twirled a strand of pale-blond hair around her finger. "But nothing crazy happened, you know? Same old, same old."

"Everyone got along well? No one seemed perturbed or annoyed?" Ellie had attended dozens of events similar to the mayor's political fundraiser, and drama never failed to play out in some corner of the room.

"I think Mrs. LaPierre got into an argument with her daughter, maybe? Like, they didn't look happy with each other, and after, the daughter disappeared for a while." Clara pursed her glossy pink lips. "I could be wrong, though. I wasn't close enough to hear what they were saying, and there was a ton of noise around the room."

Lancaster placed a heavy hand on the reception desk. "What do you mean Jackie LaPierre disappeared? For how long?"

Clara shrugged. "I don't know. I happened to be back in

the portico when that happened. Later, when I was here at my desk, I saw the daughter run out through the front door."

"Detectives." Taylor Hollback appeared behind them, clutching a folder in one hand. "I've got that information you needed. Employee names, guest list, and contacts at the catering company."

Lancaster accepted the folder. "Thanks."

Taylor produced a small thumb drive from her pocket and handed the device to Ellie. "Our IT guy put all of the video footage on it."

Ellie gripped the thumb drive in her palm. "Thanks for being so prompt. I really appreciate your help."

"No problem. Just doing my job." Taylor's cheeks flushed a hot pink. "Is there anything else we can help you with?"

Lancaster glanced at Ellie, who shook her head. "I think we're done for today, ladies. Thank you for your assistance."

Before leaving the inn, Ellie and Lancaster secured the folder and thumb drive in Lancaster's Subaru and ambled out to the rocks for a closer look. Ellie crouched above the yellow markers, her eyes drifting between the rock wall's nooks and crannies. "The report said a housekeeper found a shoe on the balcony this morning and looked over the edge. That's how they found Monique's body."

"We've had a lot of rain lately. It's a miracle the body didn't wash away in the river."

"That's what I was thinking too." Ellie navigated down on the slick rocks, a dangerous feat considering the sandals on her feet. The hem of her dress caught in a stony crevice and emerged coated in mud. *Lovely.*

Lancaster remained up top, on a rock behind her. "Forensics didn't have much to work with. The body was found a little after nine this morning. And whether she was pushed or fell last night, the water had washed away any evidence."

Ellie grabbed her skirt, wadding it in her fist to keep it tight against her legs. "Right now, we work this case as if it's a homicide."

"I agree."

Ellie balanced on a rock, unsure of whether she wanted to investigate more or return to the safety of the land above. Below her, the water rushed by, threatening to whisk her away if she made one wrong move on the slippery stones. Peering down at the yellow markers again, she searched for evidence the forensic team might've missed.

All she saw were rocks. Lots and lots of rocks. Her shoulders slumped as she turned and crawl-walked her way back to where Lancaster stood.

He leaned forward, digging the toe of his shoe into the soft, muddy grass at the side of the wall. "See anything?"

"Not real—" Ellie's toe lodged between two of the rocks, sending her sore ankle sideways. She yelped when gravity knocked her downward. The river roared beneath her, ready to yank her into its muddy clutches.

Her thoughts raced as she scrambled to regain her footing. If she wasn't around, who would take Beth in? What about her mother, who just lost a friend? And poor Clay... who would help him loosen up every now and then?

Of all the ways she might depart this world, falling into a river because her sandal slipped was not one she'd considered.

Thick fingers wrapped around her wrist, and step-by-slippery-step, Lancaster coached her back up the rocks. At the top, Ellie bent over and placed her hands on her knees to calm the heaving breaths pouring from her chest like an open water valve.

Lancaster shook his head. "Gotta be more careful, Detective Kline."

She straightened and nodded between choppy gulps of

air, massaging a red mark forming around her wrist. "Noted. Thanks for the save."

He grinned while giving her a playful nudge. "You watch my back, I'll watch yours. Did you see anything forensics missed?"

"No." Ellie scrambled up the grassy lawn, careful of her sore ankle. "Let's continue this discussion in the parking lot."

As they strode around the side of the inn, Ellie followed the irregular-shaped stepping stones to the front of the house, breathing the sweet scent of the garden's fragrant blossoms as she passed through. Lush green leaves swayed in a warm breeze. The spot was so peaceful, she contemplated perching on one of the wooden benches speckled around the garden to enjoy the silence.

"It's going to be fun trying to interview those tight-ass rich folks who think they're untouchable."

Ellie's head snapped up. *Did he really just say that to me?*

Maybe Lancaster didn't know her family was old money in Charleston. Maybe he didn't care. Either way, Ellie ignored the rude, sarcastic remark. She sped up, waltzing past Lancaster so he could stare at her back for a while. "The report said the body was found around nine this morning, but do we have a time of death yet?"

"Lobby security camera caught Monique heading up the stairs at eight twenty-seven p.m. That's the last time she was seen."

They continued in silence until they reached Lancaster's vehicle, from which Ellie retrieved the guest and employee lists. She skimmed the names. "Here's Jackie's name. Do we know what happened to her after the scene the receptionist witnessed?"

Lancaster shook his head. "We know she was there, and apparently left before all this happened. I didn't take her name off the list because, as far as I'm concerned, she's still a person of interest."

Ellie ran her finger down the rest of the list. She recognized several names. *Partridge, Rallis, Roburn, Salvatore, Kline...*

Her jaw clenched. *Kline?*

Dan Kline Jr. Her older brother. Of course he was there last night. A political fundraiser was the perfect place for him to work the crowd and dig up valuable connections he could use to further his place in their family's investment group.

Interviewing him was going to be as much fun as mowing the yard with an alligator. Sure, Lancaster could handle the questioning, but her brother was crafty and only as helpful as he wanted to be. Ellie could both weasel the facts out of him and recognize when he began spinning bullshit.

Sighing, she handed the list to Lancaster. "Could you head back to the precinct and continue following up on these names?"

He gripped the folder in his beefy fingers. "Sure. What are you going to do?"

Ellie pressed the button on her key fob. Her SUV emitted a loud *beep*. "I'm going to do what Stoddard brought me back on to do. Use my status to find out what happened to Monique LaPierre."

5

Ellie eyed the tall iron gates of the security fence framing the LaPierre property. After the guard buzzed her in, she eased her SUV down the long drive leading to the house, admiring the ancient weeping willows lining the road as she passed.

Similar to her parents' home, the house was built in a Palladian style. Two Corinthian columns stood proudly on the edges of a porch in the center of the abode. Straight rows of windows ran along most of the cream-colored exterior, save for a group of three domed windows above the front door. Four smaller roofs flanked a large, vaulted one above the columns. Classic architecture radiating grandeur.

Ellie parked her SUV in the circular driveway in front of the mansion and rang the doorbell, which was encased in an extravagant gold oval with ornate leaves.

A tiny woman dressed in a maid's uniform answered and let Ellie inside. She flipped her short black hair over her shoulder. "Please, wait here a moment. I'll get Miss LaPierre."

The housekeeper disappeared behind an arched doorway, leaving Ellie alone in the lavish foyer. Pristine marble stretched across the floor, connecting to rose-colored walls adorned with sculpted reliefs of fruits and leaves.

Bouquets of lilies, chrysanthemums, and roses covered a long entryway table near the front doors as well as much of the floor beneath. Ellie wondered if she'd find a set of sympathy flowers from her mother if she walked over and peeked at the cards.

"Ellie?"

The voice was almost less than a whisper. Ellie turned to find Jackie leaning against the doorway. "Hi, Jackie."

The Jackie in Ellie's memory was vivacious. Curvy and full of spunk. The woman in front of her, though, held none of that charm. Her skin, usually a luscious shade of sienna, was ashen and sallow. An oversize flannel shirt and yoga pants swallowed her body, and her bare feet shortened her a good inch.

"I haven't seen you since, what, your senior year?" Dark shadows lurked beneath Jackie's red-rimmed eyes. "What brings you here now?"

Ellie swallowed a lump of guilt. She and Jackie weren't super close in school, but they'd hung out more than once, thanks to their mothers' friendship. "It's been awhile, hasn't it? I came to offer my condolences and...I'm sorry, but I need to ask you a few questions."

A cough came from the room behind Jackie. Deep and rough. *A man's cough.* Ellie moved closer, pulling her newly retrieved badge from her bag.

Jackie tilted her head, her dark hair wild around her face while she eyed the official identification. "Oh, yeah. I heard you were a cop or something. Step into the drawing room. Maggie's making us some tea."

Ellie followed Jackie through the doorway into a room drenched in navy-and-gold brocade and lush burgundy carpeting. All the furniture balanced on curved and polished wooden legs. In the center of the room, tissues and wine glasses cluttered an enormous square coffee table.

A muscular man rose from an uncomfortable-looking armchair in the corner when they entered. His blond hair was cropped so close to his scalp, Ellie thought for a moment he was bald. "You okay, Jacks?" He stared at Ellie.

She stuck out a hand and introduced herself.

For such a big guy, he had a weak handshake. "Gregory Chavin. I'm sure you know this is a difficult time for Jackie."

Ellie nodded. "I know, and I'm sorry for that. But I wouldn't be here if it weren't important. I'll be as quick as I can."

Jackie shoved some throw pillows off a couch with tufted upholstery. Behind the sofa, an enormous picture window showcased the front lawn. After motioning for Ellie to sit, she eased herself onto the side nearest the man. "What do you want to know?"

The couch hardly sank when Ellie's butt hit the cushions. Crossing her legs, she angled her body toward Jackie. "The fundraiser for the mayor. Did you go with your mom last night, or did you attend the event separately?"

Jackie brushed a finger against her nose as a tear slid down. "We arrived together, but Mom and I got into a tiff pretty early in the evening. I called an Uber and left."

Ellie made a mental note to check the Uber's records and confirm the time of pickup and drop-off.

The front desk receptionist at the venue called the interaction between Jackie and her mother an argument. Much more heated than a simple quarrel.

"What was the disagreement about?"

"I don't know." Jackie leaned forward and put her head in her hands, rocking gently. "Stupid stuff. I didn't feel like being the lead puppet in our family's puppet theater. I told her I was done."

Jackie's words dripped with regret and resentment. Ellie hesitated to push her further, but getting answers was her job. She softened her tone. "Explain that to me. What puppet show?"

"Are you kidding? You know the puppet show. You're in one, too, aren't you?" Jackie did a grand sweeping motion with her hands, gesturing around the room. "This. The lavish prison that's always been my mom's life…my dad's life. I don't give a shit about the pomp and circumstance of society or keeping a death grip on the material luxuries we have. Mom was telling me to go along with it last night. Because I'm a LaPierre. Because I would tarnish my dad's good name if I didn't."

Ellie stiffened.

Jackie wasn't wrong. For many years, Ellie had played the part of good little rich girl to please her social butterfly mother. The role never fit. Rebellion bubbled inside her, egging her to lash out every chance she got. So she had.

She broke free from her mom's strings by joining the police force and defying society's perception of an heiress.

There was also Kingsley, the man who'd kidnapped her when she was younger and who'd spent years tormenting her after she escaped his clutches. He tried to make her his puppet too. Pulling her strings and, for a while, keeping her all tangled up.

But Kingsley's dead.

Ellie was no one's puppet anymore.

Dark tendrils of hair clung to Jackie's eyelashes. Rolling her eyes, she brushed the offending curls away. "Not that Dad would even care. Being dead and all."

Emotion swelled in Ellie's chest. *Poor Jackie.* Back when they were teenagers, Jackie had a chip on her shoulder about the duties and rules assigned to them, but she hadn't possessed the bitterness that tinged every word she spoke now. She'd grown so jaded over the years.

Ellie averted her gaze from her disheveled friend. She should've been there for Jackie. Instead, she'd taken off to create a new path for her own life, leaving her former friend in the dust. Guilt clogged her throat.

The housekeeper drifted into the room with a silver tray. "Excuse me."

She set a teapot, three teacups, and a plate of thin yellow cookies on the coffee table before drifting away again. Gregory leaned forward to pour himself a cup of tea. He grabbed a handful of cookies and balanced them on the armrest of the expensive-looking chair.

A throbbing ache rooted in Ellie's lower back. She twisted her shoulders, trying to discreetly stretch the muscles. "Can you tell me about your father?"

Jackie sighed and raised her glistening eyes to meet Ellie's. "I'm sure you know he died a couple of years ago. Prostate cancer. Mom was gutted when he passed. I know she would've traded the vast family fortune she received in the will in a heartbeat to spend one more day with him."

Gregory leaned over and placed a hand on Jackie's knee. A circular tattoo, about midway down his bicep, peeked out from beneath the short sleeve of his black t-shirt.

"Dad knew this wasn't me. He understood how much I hated this life. The parties, the social politics, the extravagance. I'm not a princess. The only thing I ever wanted to be was normal. He got that." With a huff, Jackie fell back against the couch cushions. "Mom, not so much."

Ellie eyed Gregory. "What about you, Mr. Chavin? How are you involved with the family?"

"Please, call me Greg." He straightened and sipped his tea. "I'm also a friend. A close one."

"He's my boyfriend. Jeez, Greg, why are you being so

weird?" There was no emotion in Jackie's words as she stared at the ceiling.

Ellie shifted in his direction. "How did you two meet?"

Greg relaxed his shoulders. "We met at the LaPierre Foundation. I was one of the troubled kids they helped."

Interesting. "Troubled? What does that mean, exactly?"

He frowned. "My parents died when I was little. After that, I got swapped in and out of foster homes. Most belonged to assholes looking for that state assistance payout who didn't care about the kids they'd agreed to look after."

"Sounds like a rough childhood."

"It was. By the time I turned eighteen, I'd already been in juvenile detention for six months." The corners of his mouth lifted. "That's when Monique found me."

Jackie turned to Ellie. "Mom got him a part-time job and enrolled him in community college."

Greg nodded. "Yeah, now I'm an associate at a local pharmacology company. Pay isn't much, so I moonlight with the White Gloves Catering Service."

Ellie blinked at the casual way he tossed out the detail. "The one handling the fundraiser? You were there last night?"

"I was on the waitstaff. It was nice. I got paid to spend the night with Jackie."

Except you didn't *spend the night with Jackie. Where were you when she and her mother fought? Or when Jackie raced away in an Uber?*

"What time did you leave?"

"Shortly after eight o'clock. I met up with some buddies for a poker game that started at eight thirty."

"Just to cover all the bases of the investigation, can you give me the names and contact information of your buddies?"

"Sure." His gaze flitted to Jackie, who remained still and quiet. "Are you okay, babe?"

Jackie's head lolled, her cheeks flushing beneath her mop of dark hair. "Ellie, I don't want to talk anymore. Can we catch up some other time? My mom just died, and I…" Tears trailed down to her chin.

"Yes, of course." Ellie rose while fumbling in her bag for a couple business cards. *I can't imagine losing my mom like she just did.* "If you think of anything that might help with the investigation, please call me. Or if you need to talk to someone. For any reason."

Greg stood and helped Jackie to her feet. "Can you let yourself out?"

"Sure." Ellie handed them both a card before trailing behind them. "Please email or text me those names as soon as you can."

In the foyer, Greg maneuvered Jackie to the stairs and guided her up, step-by-step.

Ellie continued toward the front door, turning back for one more glance at the couple as their backs disappeared into the upper floor shadows.

I'm glad she has a solid support system. She's got to be going through hell.

When Ellie climbed back into her SUV, the heat almost suffocated her. She cursed herself for forgetting to crack the windows as she cranked the AC and pressed the button to lower the windows. A warm breeze floated through the vehicle as she drove back to the main gate.

Jackie was a mess, Greg worked for White Glove Catering, and Monique and Jackie's argument was over typical mother-daughter stuff. What else had she learned during her visit?

Ellie stuck her arm out the window, balancing her elbow on the frame. Wind drifted between her fingers as she drove.

The branches of the weeping willows lining the road swayed in the breeze like they were waving farewell.

This place is truly a slice of heaven. And now the entire property and the LaPierre fortune belonged to Monique's daughter.

Jackie seemed wrecked by her mother's death. At least, she'd appeared that way during their visit. Ellie didn't want to think the worst of her friend, but money-focused situations could transform people. Greed was a powerful motive and, sadly, a common one.

Ellie's stomach knotted. She and Jackie weren't as close as they once were. Was it possible her friend had changed over the years? For the worse?

Lost in thought, she tapped her fingers against the steering wheel while she waited for the guard to buzz open the iron gates at the end of the drive. There was one sure way to get her answers and clear her friend's name from the suspect list.

She needed to go over Jackie's and Greg's alibis and background with a fine-tooth comb.

6

By the time Ellie returned to the precinct, nearly everyone had cleared out for the day. Almost. Lancaster was hunched over his desk, marking a piece of paper. He glanced up as she walked past. "Detective Kline. Was wondering when you'd show up again."

Ellie ignored the low-key sass in his voice. Dropping her bag on her desk, she plopped into her chair. The hum of the air conditioner and a couple of muffled conversations in the far corners of the station were the only disturbances to the peaceful silence in the normally chaotic communal area.

She snapped a hair band off her wrist and wrestled her unruly red locks into a ponytail. "Find anything while I was gone?"

Lancaster shrugged and placed the pencil on the desk. "I've made some calls to the employees and guests who were there last night. Getting a bit of the good old rich folk runaround. I keep pushing forward, though. Removed a few names because they either weren't there, or I've confirmed they left early."

"Let me see what you've got." Ellie stood and massaged the back of her neck on her way to his desk. Next to a few names, he'd made notes on the sheet indicating he still needed to check alibis. "Any luck with the security footage?"

"Not much." Lancaster opened his laptop. A window with the footage was loaded in the corner. After clicking to increase the video to full screen, he hit play.

Ellie leaned over his shoulder.

Lancaster pointed out Monique LaPierre as she glided through the portico of the Coastline Inn. "Here's the altercation with her daughter, and that's the last of her on film for the night."

The black-and-white footage showed Jackie pouting at the table before storming off, displaying all her hurt feelings like a thorny crown. The pained expression on Monique's face as her daughter abandoned her broke Ellie's heart.

That was the last time Jackie spoke to her mother. No wonder she was a mess when I saw her.

As Lancaster dragged his mouse, the video sped up. He paused on a suave man in a pretentious pinstripe suit, tapping the screen right over the man's face. "Monique LaPierre vanishes. Around the same time, this guy also disappears for a while. I find that a curious coincidence, don't you?"

Ellie's heart picked up speed. "It was a big event with people coming and going every second."

The male figure in question was her older brother, but Lancaster didn't need to know that. *Yet.*

Her partner stared at her, and she wondered if he already knew. After a moment, he grunted and restarted the video at the regular speed. People dancing. People drinking. People talking. No one aware of Monique LaPierre's murder happening on the other side of the building.

"Also," Lancaster slouched back in his chair and crossed his arms, "I checked out the security cameras for the third floor. They weren't malfunctioning last night."

"Then what happened to the footage?" Ellie rested her butt on the edge of Lancaster's desk.

"The system is controlled by motion capture. Someone moves near the cameras, they activate. Those cameras on the third floor never activated. Meaning, either there was no movement on the third floor at all that night, which we know isn't true, or someone monkeyed with the cameras." He tugged his shirt collar and glanced at the clock on the wall.

Ellie twirled the case file to face her and flipped through the notes. The manager of the inn gave them the head security guy's name. The one in charge that night. Where was his information?

She tapped the name. "Bernard Cookson was running security. We should chat with him about the cameras."

Lancaster stretched his arms wide and yawned. "Sure. When?"

"No time like the present." Ellie hopped off his desk and scurried to get her bag.

A warm rush of air hit her when she opened the door to the precinct parking lot. Ellie tilted her head up, squinting at the softening sun. Lancaster's shoes scuffed the ground as he dragged his feet down the hall behind her.

The day was almost over. Other detectives were home, getting ready for dinner and settling into their nighttime routines. Maybe the interview could wait until tomorrow?

No. The word smacked against the back of her brain. They needed to pursue their lead now.

She had a hard time believing that the security cameras in that particular section had gone down coincidentally. Had

Bernard Cookson risked his job by tampering with the Coastline Inn's security system?

Because if he did, Ellie was determined to find out why.

7

The empty lobby of Midland Apartments reeked of bleach. Smelled like a damn hospital and burned the inside of my nose. I yanked my baseball cap lower to shield my face. Probably unnecessary, given dumps like this rarely had security cameras. Those were for the uppity assholes around the premier river locations.

Fucking Bernard.

Pulling him in on this was not ideal. If any heat headed his way, he'd crack faster than a potato chip.

A faint rustling made me pause.

What was that?

Ducking my head, I side-eyed a doorway by a couch near the elevator. Empty.

Get it together, stupid.

Examining the room again, I checked one more time to ensure I wasn't being watched. No cameras. No people. *Good.* My shoes squeaked as I advanced toward the elevator. To avoid leaving prints, I punched the button with my elbow.

The elevator was empty too. Didn't people live in this

place? Not that I was complaining. The fewer who saw me, the better.

Stepping inside the car, I stabbed the floor button with my knuckle and waited nearly a century for the damn doors to close. Bernard and his stupid elevator that wouldn't move. I didn't want to come here and deal with this shit, but he'd left me no choice.

The car lurched upward, tossing me back against the wall. I paced and paced the moving square. *Hurry up.* I glared at the little arrow above the doors. "Hurry. The. Hell. Up."

Just as the air went stale, the elevator slammed to a stop. I stood with my nose pressed against the metal for a good forty-five seconds before the doors finally spread apart.

All this shit is taking time I don't have.

I rushed down the hall, my shoes *scrooshing* against the carpet with each hurried step. Once I reached his door, I banged on the wood.

I know you're in there.

"Bernard."

The door opened just a smidge. His pudgy face appeared through the crack, his skin slick with sweat.

"Hiya, Bernard. Let me in."

He shook his head. "What are you doing here?"

I leaned into the sliver of space separating us. "I don't have time for this shit. Let me in."

"No." He swallowed, and I could almost see the little wheels turning in his head. What a time to grow a spine. Ironic, since a security guard—especially a big, burly guy like him—should already have one, but here we were. "No. You told me to cut the cameras, and someone died. If someone was going to die, you should've let me know. Do you have any idea what you…I mean, *we've* done? The trouble I'm in because of you?"

Sick of his whining, I shoved my shoulder against the

door, slamming it open wide. "Do you know what kind of trouble *I'm* in because of *you?*"

I pushed past the meek giant and kicked the door shut behind me.

Dressed in his security guard outfit, he looked ready to leave for work. *Yeah, that's not gonna happen.* I stepped toward him, and he backpedaled farther into the living room.

For an almost middle-aged man, he sure lived in a dump. Comic books everywhere and furniture cobbled together from shit he probably found discarded in the garbage. *How pathetic.* I almost tossed him a book from his ugly bookcase creation. Until I remembered. No fingerprints. That was imperative, because I'd forgotten to pick up a pair of gloves.

Bernard hovered near the door to his balcony. "What are you doing?"

The balcony. How poetic. First Monique, now him. I released a low whistle between my teeth. Finally, my man Bernard proved useful.

I stared at the open sky behind him. Twelve floors up. That would work.

"...Mrs. LaPierre was found at nine o'clock this morning. Police are still investigating the cause of death..."

My attention darted to the television. *He's watching the damn coverage?* A bar scrolled at the bottom of the screen, claiming the police suspected homicide. Grinding my teeth, I glared. The cops should've declared Monique's death a suicide. No questions.

"You were only supposed to turn the camera sensors off for a few minutes, and only while I was up there. I wanted them to get her on video going outside but not me coming up behind her so they'd think she committed suicide. Can you even fathom how monumentally you have screwed this up for me?"

Bernard flinched as spittle flew from my lips, the words shooting out with more and more venom.

"They haven't said if it's suicide or murder yet, but they're starting to figure it out. You know they will." Bernard pointed at the news reporter. "They'll be talking about us and what we did. Everyone's going to know, and we'll both go to jail."

The rage I'd embraced while shoving Monique over the balcony returned like a lightning strike. Bernard didn't have a clue about what I'd planned for him. He still thought he'd get out of this situation alive. The knowledge almost made me smile. I'd soon experience that exhilaration again. "Turn that shit off. Now."

He scrambled to the couch and snatched a remote off the armrest. The television blipped into blackness. He tripped backward again, closer to the balcony this time. "I asked what you wanted. Why are you here?"

"Open the balcony door, Bernard."

He glanced sideways, his hand trembling. "Why?"

"Couldn't you use some fresh air? I know I could. For damn sure. Open the fucking door."

Reaching around to the back of my pants, I wrapped my fingers around the pistol stuffed in the waistband. There were two ways this could go. Messy or clean.

Bernard hesitated before unlocking the door and sliding the glass open. A hot burst of wind blasted against my face. He raised his voice enough to concern me. "Just so you know, I'm not afraid to go to the cops." Bernard's gaze flicked to the armrest on the other side of the couch, where his phone sat.

I laughed, deep and hard. No way would he reach the device in time to dial the first nine, let alone contact the operator.

Jerking the pistol from my waistband, I flicked the safety

off and aimed the weapon. Bernard's eyes widened as I motioned for him to step onto the balcony.

"It's funny, you know. Your threats." My mocking tone was thick. "'Oh, you're a bad guy. I'm going to call the police.'"

Bernard backed onto the balcony, stumbling over the sliding door track along the way. He stuttered as he spoke. "Wh…why?"

I retrieved a prepared syringe from my back pocket, ripped the cap off with my teeth, and spit the plastic into my hand. He eyed me warily as I approached, the pistol in one hand and the syringe in the other.

"The way I see it, you won't be calling anyone ever again."

8

Cars lined the curb on the street outside Midland Apartments as Ellie searched for an available spot. She passed Lancaster, who'd slid into an empty space.

What's a woman gotta do for some decent parking around here?

Irritated, she drove around the building, ducking beneath her sun visor to get a better look at the place.

The structure was older, with walls of faded bricks scaling high into the air. Sets of double windows opening to single balconies dotted the exterior. Ellie turned a corner and cruised past a tennis and basketball court situated around the back.

By the time she made her way to the front of the building again, the sun was disappearing behind a playground across the street. Trees along the sidewalk cast long, dark shadows onto the road. Lancaster reclined against the side of his car, tapping his foot and gesturing to a now-empty spot.

Ellie parallel parked behind his Subaru and hopped out of her SUV. The floaty fabric of her sundress flew up as she exited the vehicle, billowing to her upper thighs. She slapped at the skirt and slammed the door shut.

Lancaster met her on the sidewalk. "Bit of Marilyn Monroe trouble there?"

She ignored the remark. All this extra legwork? Not on her original schedule for the day. Ellie had intended to enjoy a lazy, carefree afternoon with Bethany, and she'd dressed accordingly.

Ellie headed for the main doors. "What floor is—"

Her words froze mid-sentence as a bone-chilling scream sliced through the air from high above. The sound grew louder, like a train rushing toward her at full speed.

A sickening *thud*, followed by a shattering crash, cut off the cry. As she whirled around, Ellie's heart slammed against her ribs.

The scene before her unfolded like a grotesque tableau. A blue car parked just behind her SUV had been brutally transformed into a grave of twisted metal and shattered dreams. Its roof, now a crumpled shell, had caved in under the weight of a life abruptly ended. Glass shards from the exploded windows sparkled on the asphalt as the car's alarm wailed a mournful dirge. There, amidst the chaos, sprawled a crumpled form drenched in blood, their identity obscured by the violence of their fall.

"Call for a bus," Ellie shouted as she sprinted toward the vehicle, though she knew all the paramedics in the world wouldn't be able to help.

Once she reached the gruesome site, her stomach roiled. Not from the blood and brain matter pooling like a lake, but from instant understanding.

A man. Dressed in a security guard uniform branded with the Coastline Inn logo. She reached for his twisted arm and placed two fingertips against his wrist before stepping back.

The man she'd come to interview was gone.

"Twelfth floor." Lancaster covered the mic on his phone. "Check the guard's apartment. 1205."

The strong, metallic scent of fresh blood invaded Ellie's nose. She scurried backward and pointed at Lancaster. "Wait for the ambulance and keep the scene secure until the uniforms arrive."

Lancaster sputtered a protest, but Ellie ignored him. Her sandals slapped the tile as she burst into the lobby and flashed her badge at a crowd gathered near the windows. "Charleston Police. Stay inside."

The elevator clanked all the way to the twelfth floor. Her stomach dropped as the car bounced to an abrupt stop. Ellie readied her pistol, waiting for the doors to open. When they did, several seconds later, the hallway was empty.

Creeping down the corridor, she scanned every nook and cranny. If the body smashed into the car downstairs was Bernard Cookson, and if he had something to do with Monique LaPierre's death, there was a possibility he'd just committed suicide to escape justice.

Or Monique LaPierre's *actual* killer paid Bernard a visit and silenced him. If that was the case, Ellie could be in danger. Her fingers tightened around her weapon.

1201, 1203, 1205...

She gripped her pistol in one hand and banged on the door with the other. "Charleston PD. Open up."

Somewhere down the hall, a dog barked. Ellie waited, listening closely for the slightest hint of noise from inside the apartment. No response. She pounded the wood again. "Bernard Cookson. Open up. Now."

Four units down, on the other side of the hall, a loud creak sounded, and a woman with her hair in pink and purple curlers poked her head out. She squinted at Ellie.

"Get back inside, ma'am. You aren't safe out here." She banged on the door one last time.

The woman covered her mouth and fled back into the safety of her home, slamming the door behind her.

Ellie pushed her body against the door to Bernard's apartment. The wood wasn't too thick. A powerful kick to the right weak spot and…

Crack.

The lock busted out of the frame, and the door swung against the wall before bouncing back at Ellie when she entered the apartment.

To the right, a narrow kitchen of dingy white cabinets and appliances greeted her. She hugged her weapon to her chest as she glanced inside. *Clear.* Carefully opening a closet door on the left, she found a stack of rags and a vacuum cleaner. *Clear.*

The main room was decorated in poverty-chic. A mismatched grouping of side tables surrounded a battered tweed couch. In front of it, a piece of plywood resting on red-and-blue milk crates served as a coffee table. More wood was balanced on sets of concrete blocks along the walls.

There, she found an impressive array of comic books, a few Stephen King novels, and a ton of football knickknacks filling the makeshift bookshelves. Otherwise, the main room was clear.

Two doors left.

Her shoes sank into the carpet with each step. Turning the knob of the first door, she nudged the barrier open with her foot before peeking in at a bathroom with pale-peach tiles. A white porcelain sink protruded from the wall. A toilet rested beside the sink. Stepping softly, Ellie inched closer to the shower curtain concealing the bathtub and eased the fabric back.

Clear.

One more room to go.

Holding her breath, she pushed the door open and lunged into a bedroom with a mattress on the floor. A mountain of blue-striped sheets and afghans were shoved high against the wall behind the bed. More horror novels scattered the floor. She edged her way to the closet and peered inside. A bunch of faded shirts and pants.

Clear.

Returning to the main room, she paused. Hot air swept through from the ajar glass door that led to the balcony on the opposite side of the room. Ellie stuck her head out. Plastic chairs were folded in one corner, and a leafy green plant in a sturdy terracotta pot rested in the other. There was no sign of a struggle.

The entire apartment was clear.

Dammit.

All those ifs.

As she took in the scene, a concept known as What You See Is All There Is—or WYSIATI for short—popped into her mind. The term, coined by Daniel Kahneman, examined human bias and the ways people thought when confronted with a situation. For Ellie, however, it was a reminder of how easily one could be swayed by initial appearances, focusing only on the information immediately available.

If she used the WYSIATI guidelines alone, it would be easy to reach the conclusion that Bernard killed Monique and then committed suicide. Case closed.

She didn't buy it, though.

Ellie's instincts as a detective cautioned against jumping to conclusions. Although the WYSIATI principle might explain a straightforward interpretation, her experience had taught her that the truth often lay hidden beneath the surface, especially in cases that appeared to be accidents or suicides. In this delicate balance between appearance and reality, Ellie was determined to uncover the full story, looking beyond the initial evidence to ensure no detail was overlooked.

Shit.

Her stomach dropped. Downstairs, instead of thinking through every possibility, she'd whizzed past a door for a stairwell. Had a killer escaped that way while she wasted time with the elevator? Maybe even snuck right past Lancaster as he tried to control the crime scene?

Heat burned Ellie's cheeks. She cursed herself for not being more vigilant. Instead of blindly racing upstairs in the elevator, she should've been strategic, either guarding the lobby herself or assigning someone to monitor the stairwell exit. Keeping track of everyone who came down was crucial, and she had missed it.

Rubbing her temples, she stalked out of the apartment.

Double dammit!

9

By the time Ellie and Lancaster returned, darkness had settled over the precinct. Ellie perused a takeout menu in the break room, relieved her mother had offered to care for Bethany. Sighing, she tossed the menu aside. Dinner would have to wait until after she and Lancaster finished the paperwork on the victim at Midland Apartments.

Lancaster munched on a pastry from the vending machine while looking over papers fanned out on his desk as Ellie approached. The sugary sweet scent of strawberry got her tastebuds salivating.

Her stomach groaned in hunger. She wrapped an arm around her belly and hoped Lancaster didn't hear the growl. "What've we got?" She pulled a chair up and sat beside him.

He brushed crumbs off his shirt. "Well, the victim who took a nosedive onto the car has been confirmed as Bernard Cookson."

"I figured."

The empty apartment with the balcony door open, the uniform belonging to the Coastline Inn…

Who else could it have been?

After the ambulance arrived, Ellie and Lancaster had split up to talk to residents and staff at the apartment building. Three hours later, they were back at the station and no closer to any answers.

Lancaster scratched his bald head. "I mean, this screams suicide. He played some part in Monique's death, hell, maybe even was the one who murdered her. We've got an apartment with a locked door and no sign of forced entry. Except yours."

The jab didn't sit well with Ellie. She bit her inner cheek and exhaled slowly. "His place was locked up tight when I got there. We didn't find his keys, though. It's possible the killer took them. He could've locked the door behind him to tie everything up into a nice bow. There wasn't an internal dead bolt or chain, so the whole scene looks self-explanatory."

"Yep. Pretty cut and dried. Especially if we can pin Monique LaPierre's murder on him." Lancaster yawned and tossed his empty pastry wrapper into a bronze-colored trash can under his desk.

Ellie blinked a few times. Was he trying to imply they should pin Monique's murder on Bernard and call it a day? Shivers pricked at her skin. She rose from her chair. "Why don't you let me go over the list of guests and employees for a while?"

He waved dismissively. "I'm fine. Don't worry. Most of the names are crossed off anyway. I've been conducting interviews over the phone and eliminating suspects that way. Saves a hell of a lot of time."

The shivers sank into Ellie's bones, shooting tingles up and down her body. "Wait, that's how you're clearing the list? Just giving people a call isn't good enough."

Lancaster huffed. "Detective Kline, we don't have time to

invite every upper-class Tom, Dick, and Harry down to this station for tea and a chat. The list was given to me, I'm handling it, and I don't need your help."

Ellie raised her voice. "You can't read people over the phone. You can't get under their skin. Anybody can lie their ass off on the phone."

"You know what?" Lancaster slammed his laptop shut and shoved the device into a leather bag. He dropped the list into a desk drawer and locked the cabinet up with a key on his key ring. "I think I'm done for today. I'll see you tomorrow, Detective Kline."

Her body burned with rage. She fumed as he stomped away. The whole partner thing? Ellie was over being saddled with one.

A cough echoed from the hall. Ellie jerked her head and marched toward Stoddard's office. She flung the door open with more force than intended, causing the handle to clang against the concrete wall.

Stoddard's head shot up. "Kline! What the actual hell?"

"How long?" Ellie stormed into the room. "How long do I have to put up with Lancaster? He's slowing me down. I do my best work solo."

"Having to play nice with a partner is what has you all twisted up in knots?" Stoddard scoffed and settled back in her chair. "My hands are tied. The assigned partner is a condition of your reinstatement. At least for the short term."

"Then I want another one."

"Not happening." Stoddard pointed a pen at her. "No one else was willing to work with you, Kline. You've got a reputation in this department. People think you're a hotshot who gets way too many second chances. On top of that, you're an aggressive, strong woman in a department filled with men who are intimidated by aggressive, strong women.

Lancaster was the only detective willing to butt heads with you for this case."

What?

Ellie floundered for a response, uncertain if she should riff on the hotshot comment or blush from Stoddard's assessment of her. She crossed her arms. "My job is to solve crimes, not make friends."

Stoddard's expression hardened. "That's your problem. You can't cross the bridges you've burned, and you've burned quite a few. I think this is a chance for you to learn how to work with others. Nobody can do everything on their own. Not me, not Lancaster, and not you. We have to work together. The requirement stands. Accept it."

Ellie dug her nails into her palms, stilted breaths catching in her lungs. She could walk away. Slam the badge and gun she'd just gotten back onto Stoddard's desk and leave. Ignore Stoddard's calls from now on and spend time with her family instead.

Why did she keep subjecting herself to this childish bullshit? The boys didn't want to play with her because she was better than them, and Stoddard used her higher rank to discredit her whenever she could. Why stay?

The pressure in her fingertips relaxed, and her breathing stabilized. Ellie stayed because the job was bigger than her and Stoddard and the other detectives. She'd sworn to protect the people of Charleston and, when she couldn't protect them, get them justice.

Breaking that promise wasn't an option.

She squared her shoulders. "Fine."

The word was terse and didn't address any of the myriad issues Ellie faced with Stoddard. It was, however, enough in the moment. She turned and raced down the hallway, stopping at her desk for a split second to retrieve her bag and keys.

Did she want a partner? No. Did she have to work with one in order to keep her promise to the people of Charleston? Yes. So she would.

For now.

10

The night sky was a deep shade of navy sprinkled with a smattering of stars. Ellie admired them as she sipped a glass of wine on the deck of her parents' house. The breeze was balmy, and the workday was over. She had alcohol, her mom's chef was whipping up a quick meal in the kitchen, and her boyfriend was on his way over to share a late dinner.

Could life get any better?

The door behind her slid open and closed. Helen Kline joined her by the railing. "Louis says the steak and potatoes are almost ready. Why don't you come on inside?"

With a nod, Ellie followed her mother into the sunroom and down the lavish hall into the dining room, embracing her before sitting at the table. "I'm so sorry about Monique, Mom."

Helen pressed her fingertips to her temples. "You've said that to me a dozen times since you got here."

On any other case, talking to the friends and family of a victim was difficult but doable. Now her mom was that friend or family member. Ellie kept trying, but the right words to ease her mother's pain eluded her. "It's just, I know you guys had been friends for several years and this is hard for you."

A sad smile emerged, and her mother's dark-brown eyes glistened beneath the chandelier crystals. "Decades. We'd been good friends since before you and Jackie were even born."

Her mother, already a petite woman next to Ellie's five-ten, appeared shriveled in the wake of her friend's death. Grief paled her peaches and cream complexion. Even her usually vibrant red hair looked dull.

Bethany ran into the room and laced her fingers through Helen's. "Nana, I lost you."

Ellie's mother bent over to wrap the child in a hug. She glanced at Ellie. "Thank you for letting this one stay over tonight. She's been such a huge help."

"Yeah?" Ellie grinned at Bethany. "Have you been taking good care of Nana?"

Bethany nodded and held up their intertwined fingers. "I haven't let go of her hand since I got here because she's sad, and she said me holding her hand makes her feel better. Oh, wait." The little girl tapped a finger on her chin.

The doorbell rang. Ellie spied Eustace, the family butler, shuffling past to answer the call.

Ellie grinned at the child. "Wait for what?"

"I forgot I had to let go of your hand when I went to the bathroom. And when Chef Louis gave me apple sticks and cheese. And when Ellie got here and I hugged her…" Bethany's face lit up. "Clay!"

Clay Lockwood ruffled Bethany's blond hair. "Hey, kiddo." The bright blue of his polo shirt accentuated the tan he'd gotten from days spent fishing and hiking. Warm strands of chestnut swam in his mahogany hair. When he grinned at her, his cheeks, sprinkled with a hint of sunburn, bubbled out.

Ellie returned the gesture, thrilled to have her boyfriend back. While she and her family had come back from their vacation in Long Field Township a couple days ago, Clay stayed behind to spend some one-on-one time with his sister, Caraleigh. He also couldn't leave until the hood of his Bronco, damaged in an altercation with the Long Field killer, was repaired.

Refusing to let go of her nana's hand, Bethany dragged Ellie's mother over to greet Clay as well.

Though Helen smiled, the gesture didn't last long. "Good evening, Clay."

"Helen." Clay rested his palm on her shoulder. "I'm so sorry to hear about your friend."

She patted his hand. "Thank you. Come, sit. Louis is making a little something for you too."

Clay kissed the top of Ellie's head as he scooted behind to take a seat next to her. "Hey, you."

Ellie tilted her head and smiled, slightly buzzed and happy to be surrounded by the people she loved.

Eustace appeared in the doorway, balancing a silver tray holding two plates of garlic butter steak with a side of fried potatoes, as well as a glass of water for Clay. He placed the plates and beverage in front of the couple.

The meat's smoky scent shot Ellie's taste buds into overdrive. Saliva pooled in the corners of her mouth as if she were a ravenous bear. Without remorse, she liberated the fork and knife from the neatly folded napkin and sliced away at the steak, eager for the salty and buttery juices to swim between her teeth and dive down her throat.

"Ellie didn't provide many details on your friend." Clay stuck his fork into a thick chunk of steak and bit into the cut. "If you have some stories you'd like to share, I'm all ears."

"Oh, Monique had a heart of gold. Always trying to help people, especially children." Helen tapped the table with her finger. "It's not really talked about, but her daughter is adopted."

"What?" Ellie almost dropped her fork. Maybe she'd had too much to drink. "Jackie LaPierre? Adopted?"

Helen nodded and dragged a fingertip over the lip of her water glass. "Yes. Jackie must've been six or seven months old at the time. Hal and Monique visited Brazil to discuss plans for a possible satellite location of their foundation. The proposed land already had an orphanage on it. They were down there a couple of months, Hal negotiating and Monique sightseeing. In the end, Hal chose not to expand but did send regular donations to the orphanage and provided scholarships for the children. And, when they returned, they brought Jackie back with them."

Wow.

"Does she know she's adopted?" Ellie couldn't recall Jackie ever mentioning that.

Helen chuckled. "Of course. Hal and Monique didn't hide the truth from her. Honestly, Eleanor, I think the whole expansion story was bunk. Monique was so excited before that trip. And adopting from Brazil makes sense. Monique's mother was from Brazil, so Monique often visited the country while growing up."

Ellie lifted a forkful of tender steak and fried potatoes to her mouth, savoring the rosemary and salt on her tongue. Her stomach settled, relieved to finally be fed.

"So does Jackie inherit all the money?" Clay scooped a potato and a seared sliver of steak onto his fork.

The money. A solid motive for murder. During her visit earlier to the LaPierre mansion, Ellie found Jackie full of resentment regarding her family's fortune. Was all of her griping an act? Jackie was now the sole heir to the entire LaPierre estate.

"Yes. Hal died a couple of years ago. Prostate cancer.

Monique took things over after his death. She was considering a new project to raise money for cancer, in honor of Hal, but I don't think the idea got very far with the LaPierre Foundation."

Clay froze, his fork halfway to his mouth. "Did you say the LaPierre Foundation? Your friend was Monique...LaPierre?"

Ellie clocked the way his jaw twitched at the name. Like a trigger response. "Have you been under a rock today? It's been all over the news."

"I spent most of today in Long Field getting my vehicle back from the shop and hanging out with Caraleigh and Luke in their backyard." Clay shrugged. "I was still in rest-and-relax mode. Didn't spend a bunch of time checking the news."

"I guess that's a valid reason." After a playful nudge to his arm, she raised her wine glass and took a sip. "You've been volunteering there for a long time, haven't you, Mom?"

"Yes, I honestly can't remember a time when I wasn't involved."

"What do they do?" Clay's question was innocent enough, but Ellie picked up on the way he slowed his movements to focus on her mother's words.

"It's a charity-focused nonprofit designed to help troubled youths escape impossible situations." Helen tilted her head and frowned. "Hal lost a best friend as a child. The kid couldn't seem to dig his way out of trouble. When he died, Hal never forgave himself. He pledged to do what he could to prevent the same thing from happening to others. And the LaPierre Foundation was born."

Bethany rested her head on Helen's arm and yawned, still gripping her nana's hand. "What's a lap hair?"

Helen patted her head and rose, rousing the sleepy child to move with her. "I suppose I should get this one to bed."

Ellie set her wine glass on the table. "Do you need help?"

Her mother shook her head. "No. I'll be fine, really. I might just fall asleep up there with Bethany. Just come check on me before you leave. Good night."

The moment Bethany's door closed, Clay turned to Ellie. "On the phone earlier today, you said Stoddard reinstated you at the Charleston PD. Are you working the LaPierre case?"

"Yes." Ellie gestured to the hunks of meat and potatoes still on his plate. "Are you going to eat the rest of that?"

He slid the dish toward her. "Is there anything I can do to help with the investigation?"

Ellie stopped shoveling his leftovers into her mouth and eyed him with suspicion. "Why?" Though Clay usually helped on her cases, this unsolicited volunteering of his services piqued her curiosity.

"Does it matter?"

After considering his question, she decided it didn't. "Not right now. But I'll let you know if that changes. Things are really just getting ramped up."

"Keep me posted." Clay pressed a linen napkin to his mouth before tossing the fabric onto the table. "Your poor mom. She's being strong, but it feels like there's a lot of hurt simmering under the surface."

Ellie set her fork down and stacked the plates on top of each other. She fiddled with the ridge gliding along the edge of the top plate. "Mom's strong. She doesn't like to show her emotions, but I know she'll get through this."

"Are you certain she's that strong?"

Ellie couldn't answer that question. Not honestly. Her mom had been through a lot. She'd even survived Kingsley. Twice, if you counted the trauma she endured when he kidnapped a teenage Ellie. More recently, he'd used Ellie's mother as bait to lure Ellie into a trap. No doubt, Helen Kline was forged from steel.

But how much is too much?

After a moment of silence, Clay cleared his throat. "Did you know Monique well?"

"No, but the LaPierre Foundation has deep roots here in Charleston. I'm pretty sure its philanthropic mission is solid."

Clay flinched. "Pretty sure? Do you think there's a possibility Monique died because of her connection to the foundation?"

"I don't know yet."

Ellie's mind wandered around the roller coaster of an afternoon she'd experienced. All of the emotions and stumbles. She was back on the force but working at half speed thanks to being weighed down with a partner. Monique LaPierre was dead, Jackie LaPierre was adopted, and the buzz from her wine was wearing off.

Worst of all, she didn't know how to fix her mother's broken heart. Thank goodness for Bethany.

She rose and wrapped her arms around Clay's neck. "It's late. Bethany's sleeping over here. Why don't we head back to my place and celebrate you coming home?" She bent down to kiss his soft, warm lips.

They still tasted like steak.

11

Ellie poured piping hot coffee into a cup and set the container on the counter. Unlatching the top of a silver canister next to the coffee maker, she peeked inside. One packet of sugar left.

Grumbling, she opened cabinet doors and scrutinized the shelves for reinforcements. None in sight. *Damn.* She let the doors fall shut and grabbed the lone packet in the canister. Ripping a corner off, she stirred the sweetener into the liquid, watching the crystals dissolve in an instant.

The music of a news alert caught her ear. She peered into the kitchen's adjoining break room where a television hanging in the corner displayed a prim-looking woman with a white-blond bob on the screen.

Wait, I know her.

The woman's rigid body was positioned in front of several microphones. An exaggerated scowl darkened her face, but Ellie doubted the sincerity of the woman's anger. The shimmer of excitement sparkling in her eyes belied her emotions.

A breaking news banner scrolled beneath the woman as she spoke. *Monique LaPierre murdered...*

Ellie hurried into the break room, blowing into her cup to cool her drink. There, Officer Davis sat staring at the screen.

"Hey, can you turn the volume up a little?"

She gazed at the TV while Officer Davis obliged. Donna. Donna Montague. That was the woman's name. Another one of Charleston's wealthy elite. She had to be on the guest list for the black-tie event where Monique died.

Donna dabbed her eyes with a handkerchief. *"Monique was a beautiful soul. Her efforts in the community have saved countless lives. Someone took this wonderful person from us. I swear, I will leave no stone unturned in the search for her killer."* She pounded her chest, Céline Dion style.

A voice from off-screen rose above the murmuring crowd. The camera panned to a man wearing a media pass badge around his neck and holding out a tape recorder. *"Can we get more information on the reward?"*

When the camera panned back to her, Donna nodded before locking her dark-brown eyes onto the camera. *"I'm offering a reward of one hundred thousand dollars to anyone with information that will help us catch Monique's killer. We will find the person who did this, and they will pay for their heinous crime."*

Ellie rolled her eyes and huffed, tightening her grip on her cup. All that would do was spur a flood of calls that'd have them running around chasing dead ends.

Whirling out of the break room, she beelined for Lancaster's desk. "Can I see the guest list?"

He rifled through several papers, pulled one out, and handed her the sheet. Setting her cup on the edge of the desk, she grabbed the page and searched the names.

"What're you looking for?"

She pointed at Donna Montague's name. "This woman

right here. She just went on television and broadcast to all of Charleston that she's offering a one-hundred-thousand-dollar reward to anyone with information on Monique LaPierre's murder."

Lancaster shot forward. "What the…doesn't she realize that fielding all those useless calls to the tip line is going to muck up our investigation?"

Ellie sank into a chair beside him. "Maybe she does. Maybe she killed Monique and is trying to muddy the waters."

"You think?"

She scoffed. "No. Not really."

Ellie picked up the pile of documents and thumbed through them before pulling out the paper with the White Gloves Catering employee list.

Lancaster side-eyed her. "I've gone through those already."

Ellie ignored him and ran her finger down the list until she reached Gregory Chavin's name. "Did you confirm his alibi? He's apparently dating Jackie LaPierre."

"Oh, yeah? I'm still working on a few more confirmations, but so far, his alibi checks out. He left work at eight o'clock that night, half an hour before Monique even went upstairs." Lancaster yawned, showcasing his pearly whites.

She tapped several names highlighted in yellow. "What about these people? Anything interesting pop up on them?"

"Those eight have been in trouble before." He gestured to a name near the top. "Especially this guy. Lou Cramer. Has a long rap sheet and spent six months behind bars."

Ellie perused the list. "Interesting. Why are so many young men and women with criminal backgrounds working for White Gloves Catering?" *And do the company's rich, elite clients know?*

Lancaster shrugged. "Don't know. I'm still working through the employee list. Maybe I can find out."

"Good. Keep at it. I need to go check on a few things." Ellie grabbed her phone and slipped out of the room.

The oily odor of fried fish, freshly reheated from the kitchen microwave, permeated the hallway. Salmon, if she had to guess. She held her breath all the way to the elevator.

The old elevator whined as its gears and cables lowered Ellie to the basement. She nibbled her thumbnail the whole way down, deep in thought. Normally, she'd make this trip to visit with her roommate and best friend, Jillian, who worked as the evidence room clerk. But ever since Ellie's reassignment from cold cases to homicide, her visits to the archives happened less and less.

An aspect of the case nagged at her. *Something to do with the cold case files. Something I read or saw.*

LaPierre. Sure, the name belonged to family friends, but another connection teased the back of her brain. A connection she struggled to recall.

"Hey, you." When Ellie exited the elevator, Jillian Reed stood up behind the evidence room's front window, which only revealed her petite five-three frame from the neck up. She flashed Ellie a bright smile. "Haven't seen you down in these parts for a while."

Ellie punched in the code to open the door. "I've got a case that's giving me flashbacks. Thought I'd revisit the archives and try to figure out why."

She allowed herself five minutes to chat with Jillian before heading into the inner archives room. Falling into long conversation with her best friend was too easy, and any more time than that would lead to complete derailment from her mission.

Once inside, Ellie scoured the metal shelves and cardboard boxes. One by one, she lugged white boxes from the shelves to the table in the corner, removing the lids and rifling through the files—gaining a papercut or two in the process.

Ten boxes in, she glanced at her watch. She'd made plans to meet her brother for lunch at an Italian place downtown, and she still wanted to touch base with a few of the other guests who'd been at the party before the day was done. She returned the box she'd been digging through and headed out.

The files could wait.

❋

Rosarito's, the family-owned Italian restaurant her brother chose, was high class. Diners milled around the polished mahogany bar and several round, white-cloth-lined tables. Most people sported tailored dress suits and pencil skirts. A couple of touristy family types chowed down on plates of lasagna in the back, but most of Rosarito's clientele screamed upper-class management. A scent of oregano and garlic drifted through the air.

Ellie peeked down at her black chino pants and striped Ann Taylor flutter sleeve top. *I am so underdressed for this.* Sighing, she scanned the restaurant for her brother.

"Table for one?" A middle-aged woman with long black hair and a gray pinstripe vest approached her.

Once Ellie spotted Dan at a table near a window, she sidestepped the hostess and waved. "No, thank you. I'm meeting that guy."

She scuttled into the dining area and zigzagged around tables until she reached her brother.

"Ellie." Dan half rose from his chair as she sat down across from him. A basket of bread covered by a green cloth rested in the middle of the table. "Would you care for a glass of wine?"

"No. Thanks." She slid into the chair and reached for a piece of hot, fluffy bread.

"You sure?" He raised his glass and tipped it slightly. "This place has the best red I've tasted in ages. Not as good as Alfredo alla Scrofa in Rome, of course, but not bad."

Ellie frowned, wishing she were breaking bread with Wesley instead of Dan. Her little brother's laid-back attitude meant they laughed a ton when they were together. Also, he would've picked the hot dog food truck parked down the street to meet, not a stuffy place like Rosarito's. But the last time she'd spoken to him he was heading to someplace in Europe to "reconnect with nature."

She smoothed out the linen in her lap, trying her hardest to mask her annoyance. "Again, no. I'm on duty."

Dan *tsk-tsk*ed her. "I have to go back to the office too. That's not stopping me. You should live a little." He swirled his wine and took a sip.

"It's a little different for me. They really frown on police detectives getting sloshed on government time." She reached out to grab another piece of bread.

"Fine. What did you want to meet for?" Dan cocked his head. "Something with Mom and Dad? Is everything okay with Dad's heart?"

"Nothing like that. Mom's just having a difficult time right now." Ellie dipped her bread into a puddle of olive oil and parmesan. She guessed her brother probably hadn't spoken to their mother since Monique LaPierre died. "One of her good friends passed away. Have you checked in on her in the last day or two?"

Dan cleared his throat, feigning interest in the gold cuff link fastened to his crisp shirt. "I…will. This afternoon. I'd heard about Monique, but honestly, I'm not good with this stuff."

Join the club.

"Well, please try to check in on her today. She's acting strong, but I'm worried she's going to crack."

"I said I will." Dan dropped his wrist and lifted his lips in a partial smile. "How's the adoption process going?"

Ellie sighed and tore off another piece of bread. *Does he really care, or is he just trying to change the subject?*

The truth was, she questioned her ability to be a good mother to Bethany. All the time. When she braided Bethany's hair. When she corralled the little girl into a bath before bed. When they settled in to catch a movie on the couch.

Ellie cast her gaze across the table.

Dan was trying to tear the server's attention away from a couple with several questions about the menu.

Keep it simple. Getting into deep conversation with her brother about her fears of motherhood was not the point of the meeting. "Slow. It's frustrating how long the whole thing takes."

"Yes, yes. There's probably a mountain of paperwork that has to be done." Dan checked his watch. "Do you know what you want? I've got a meeting at three, so we'll need to order as soon as the server detaches from those two."

"It's only noon. How long do you think it takes me to eat?"

"That's not the problem. You'll inhale your meal." Dan poured himself another glass of wine. "I need time to digest my food and sober up."

"Ha ha." Again, she pined for her youngest brother's companionship. She made a mental note to give Wesley a call once she solved the case.

While I'm here, I might as well see if he knows anything about that photo of Dad and Francis.

"Since we're talking about family, I have a question for you. It's weird, though."

"Sure. Shoot."

Ellie leveled her gaze, eager to gauge her brother's reaction. "I've been taking Bethany to therapy, and Francis Varner, the psychiatrist she's seeing, had a photo of him and Dad in his office."

Dan shrugged and nibbled his bread. "Dad has a lot of friends. That's not so strange."

"They were both in camouflage. It looked like a military photo from abroad, like they were both in the Army together or something."

"What?" Dan coughed and whacked his chest. "Our father? In the Army? That's ridiculous."

Ellie's shoulders slumped. Judging from Dan's response, he was as in the dark about their father's past as she was. "So as far as you know, Dad was never in the military?"

"Um, no. This is the first time I've heard anything about him being even remotely involved in any branch of the military. Dad? A G.I. Joe?"

Ellie pursed her lips. *Another dead end.*

The server appeared at their table. "Welcome to Rosarito's. I apologize for the wait." He shot a sidelong glance at the couple at the other table. "What would you like this afternoon?"

Dan ordered the chicken parmigiana, while Ellie opted for the fried cheese. The server took their menus and disappeared.

"Is that what you needed to talk with me so urgently about? We could've handled that over the phone." Dan bit into another piece of bread and sipped his wine.

Right. Down to business.

"No. I want to talk about the fundraiser you went to the other night. The one for the mayor. I saw you on the security footage…except for a few minutes when you weren't. Right around the time Monique LaPierre disappeared."

"Heh?" Dan brushed breadcrumbs off his designer shirt.

"So this is an interrogation? You called me out of the office to cross-examine me? Do you know how busy I am, Ellie?"

She waved a hand. "Of course not. This isn't an interrogation. I'm just trying to gather information. Did you notice anything unusual that night?"

"No. It was a normal, boring event. When I left, I didn't know it was going to become such a hot topic. I was shocked when I found out what happened. That poor woman, lying dead on the rocks, while everyone else blew air kisses at each other and drove away. I felt awful knowing I'd been privy to such callousness."

Ellie poured cold water from a carafe into her empty glass. "Did anyone else there have an issue or conflict with Monique?"

His forehead wrinkles deepened. "How would I know? All I observed was typical party stuff. Mostly. I noticed Monique giving one server a hard time."

Ellie carefully set the pitcher back on the table. "How so? What did you see?"

"I was on my way to the restroom, so I didn't see much. Monique and the guy were having a pretty heated private discussion." Dan's shoulders rose. "I assumed she was upset about a food allergy or something. After that, I didn't see the server for the rest of the night. She might've gotten him removed."

"What did the server look like?"

Dan closed one eye and rubbed a knuckle under his chin. After a second, he shrugged. "Honestly, I was tipsy and concerned about getting to the restroom in time. I couldn't tell you anything about him. When I passed by, I hardly noticed him."

Damn.

"What about Donna Montague? What was she up to that night?"

Her brother scowled and picked up his wine glass. "What a spotlight queen. That woman will do anything to be on the society page. Even at the expense of a dead friend. Did you hear about the reward?"

Ellie nodded.

Dan smirked. "Between her and her little boyfriend, you'd think she'd want to shy away from prying eyes a bit more."

"Boyfriend?" Ellie leaned forward, her interest piqued. "What boyfriend? Isn't she married?"

"Does that matter? You know how these things go. Marriage gets a little stale, in comes the younger lover. Donna's is a good thirty years younger than she is. Her husband doesn't seem to give two flips about the affair. The entire thing is so basic. One of those rich-people problems." Dan winked, the humor in his eyes unmistakable. "Speaking of, will you be joining me at Retro tonight? I'm having some drinks with friends."

She rested her elbows on the table. "Oh? What's the occasion?"

A nightclub was the last place Ellie planned to be that evening. *Pounding noise and body heat? Pass.*

"New promotion at work." Dan waggled his eyebrows.

Ellie laughed. "Congrats on the promotion, and thanks for the invite, but I've got stuff to do tonight."

"Don't you always?" He swirled his wine before downing the rest of it.

You bet your ass.

12

Italian cuisine was not my favorite. All the heavy pasta, the acidic red sauces, and the ungodly amount of garlic used in the dishes? My stomach wouldn't handle that. So of course an Italian restaurant was the place the redheaded detective ducked into after leaving the precinct.

When I stepped through the dark glass doors of Rosarito's, I almost puked. The place reeked of spices, making my nose itch and my gut roil.

I wasn't a bland guy. Give me spicy tacos or chicken wings any day. I'd wolf those bad boys down. Italian seasonings were my kryptonite, though.

On top of that, the restaurant was for fancy types. Luckily, I'd dressed up a little today. Polo shirt and a nice pair of dress pants. Definitely classier than the tank tops and baseball caps I spotted on a couple with three kids at the back of the room.

"Would you like a table, sir?" The hostess gave off a ritzy vibe in her striped suit pants and vest, but I noticed the hole where her nose ring normally lived and the butterfly tattoo on the inside of her thumb. No doubt she was a party girl, trying to pay the bills by bowing to the high and mighty.

"No."

Dipping past her, I headed to the bar. A bartender in a vest similar to the chick's placed a bowl of toasted ravioli in front of me. I ordered an IPA and gulped the first half of the drink down in no time flat. After, I craned my neck and scanned the room.

There she was, chatting away with some fancy dude at one of the tiny tables.

Lifting the beer bottle to my lips, I took another swig, relishing the hoppy flavor as the cold brew hit my tongue. She was getting too close to figuring something out. *Fucking Bernard.* If he'd manipulated the cameras the way I explained to him, in detail and at least three times that night, I wouldn't be in this mess.

They seemed close, the detective and the dude. Closer than a cop and a witness. I concentrated on drowning out all the noise, homing in on bits and pieces of their conversation. Family. Parents. Rich people bullshit.

The man angled his head my way. *Shit.* I'd seen that profile before. At the mayoral fundraiser. The detective was talking to a witness from the party.

Just freakin' perfect. Dammit.

I shoved my quivering hand under the edge of the bar, gripping my knee to try and steady my nerves. The beer in my belly threatened to rush back up. I slugged the rest down as I gave myself a mental pep talk.

Calm down. The dude was a witness. She interrogated witnesses. All normal. *He was sloshed, too, when he passed Monique and me the other night. Very sloshed.* I doubted she'd get any useful information from him.

I curled my fingers into a fist as unwelcome memories from my past resurfaced. I'd needed the police once. No, *more* than once. I was scared. People hurt me. Used me. Where were the police then?

Nowhere in sight.

"Can I get you another?" The bartender's beard wiggled as he spoke.

Leaning over the counter, I lowered my voice. "Sure. And, hey, that man at the table over there looks familiar, but I can't place him. Any idea who he is?"

The bartender cocked his head and scoffed. I wanted to rip his smug face off by the ears. "You mean Dan Kline? Are you from out of town? His family's one of the most influential groups in Charleston."

I shot the arrogant fellow a curt smile. "Thanks, yeah, now I remember."

Kline? Wasn't that the redhead's name too? I chuckled to myself. What rotten luck. The one person who could link me to Monique that night was not only talking to the police, he was a relative. What was he, her brother? Cousin?

You just need to take care of him. Like Bernard. I'd calculated all the risks before I killed Monique, and Dan Kline didn't fit into the equation.

Unless...

Unless I killed two birds with one stone. Even from a distance, the detective seemed to care about the guy. And he knew a secret I didn't want him to reveal. I could use their relationship to my advantage.

Dan Kline needed to die.

My secret would be safe, and the detective would be so distraught over his death that her investigation would falter.

Two birds. One stone. I win.

My belly growled. After slapping a few bills on the bar, I left. The moment I stepped outside, I inhaled the fresh air, happy to free my lungs of the oregano dust floating around the restaurant.

Glancing around, I perused my lunch options. A hot dog truck sat on the corner, and a deli a little way down from that. Or I could catch a bite at the burger place three streets over.

The food didn't matter, really. More important was that I couldn't think on an empty stomach. And I was about to do a lot of thinking.

Dan Kline was going to meet an untimely end.

I just needed to figure out how.

13

A puff of frigid air hit Ellie when she pushed open the glass door to the lobby of Broadside Insurance Company. Sunlight spilled into the area through wide windows positioned along the front of the building. A trio of puffy armchairs on thin, wooden bases sat beside a desk in the corner. Behind the desk, a skinny man with a horseshoe mustache marked papers with a pen.

Ellie approached, clearing her throat to capture the man's attention. Donna Montague, the chief financial officer of Broadside Insurance Company, had offered a generous and out-of-the-blue reward to anyone who could provide information on Monique's murder. Ellie wanted her to explain why she was so invested in what happened to Monique. From what she knew of the society circle, the two were merely acquaintances. Donna's reason for shelling out a hundred grand of her own money for tips eluded Ellie.

"I'd like to speak with Donna Montague." She rubbed a hand over her chest. The fried cheese she'd eaten at Rosarito's was giving her a wild case of heartburn.

The receptionist glanced up with a frown. "Do you have an appointment?"

An earpiece clung to his left ear. It was connected to a thin wire that draped down his body and jerked straight with his movement.

"No. But I'm with the Charleston Police Department." Ellie flashed her badge. "That should get me a meeting with her, right?"

The receptionist rolled his eyes and sighed. He pushed a button on the lower end of the wire and turned away from Ellie. When he faced her again, he nodded while pressing a button underneath the desk. A door opened to the far left. "Go on in. But be aware that Mrs. Montague is a very busy woman."

"Understood. Thanks." Ellie passed through the doorway and entered a small suite.

She expected the room to be filled with luxurious furniture and decor. Donna was one of Charleston's richest women, after all. Instead, the office contained little furniture aside from a table, desk, and a couple file cabinets that lined the wall. A vase of flowers wilted over the side of another file cabinet next to a floor-to-ceiling window showcasing the city.

A young guy sat at a round meeting table eating lunch from a takeout tray from the deli next to Broadside. He was clean-shaven, his black hair tucked neatly behind his ears, and oozed smarm. Bulging muscles threatened to burst the seams of his tight, baby blue button-down. When his gaze landed on Ellie, he licked his greasy lips and ran his dark gaze up and down her body.

Is that the boyfriend?

He stuck a chip in his mouth and sucked on the crispy flake, his eyes glued to her chest. *Blech.* She shifted her attention to Donna, wishing the creepy boy toy would leave.

While in her sixties, Donna's features still possessed a youthfulness that belied her age. Her white-blond hair hung loose around her shoulders in a short bob. Years of moisturizer, massages, and more than a little plastic surgery kept the crow's feet and smile lines at bay.

Donna was perched behind a wide desk, her long fingernails *clack-clacking* against her laptop keyboard. The vibrant, purple silk tunic she wore complemented the porcelain color of her skin. She stopped typing as Ellie entered the room. "Quint, skedaddle for a while, okay? Detective Kline and I need to chat for a bit."

The boy toy shrugged before gulping down the rest of his soda. He picked up the tray of remaining food and rose from the table, tossing a lecherous grin Ellie's way as he sauntered past her. The fabric of his dress pants *swished* between his thighs with each step.

Internally, Ellie shuddered, goose bumps rising on her arms.

Donna motioned Ellie forward and shoved her laptop aside. "Come sit, dear. I know your mother. How is she doing with this nasty business? She and poor Monique were close, weren't they?"

"She's doing okay." Ellie eased into a chair in front of Donna's desk and set her bag on the floor. "It's still very raw, of course. But she's making it through, day by day."

"Such a strong woman. And such a treasure for our community. Her charity has a big milestone coming up soon. Forty years or something?" Donna folded her hands together and balanced her chin on her knuckles.

Ellie crossed her legs. "Yes. The fortieth anniversary is in a couple weeks." Kline House, her mother's project, was a big deal for the community. The charity provided support to people who'd lost their homes in fires and other disasters, but Ellie wasn't here to discuss her mother's contributions to the populace. "You were at the mayor's fundraiser the other night. And the party afterward."

"Eh?" Donna dropped her hands and leaned back in her seat, drumming her manicured nails on the desktop. "You get straight to the point, don't you? No chitchat. Okay. How can I help you?"

"By answering my questions honestly. How did you know Monique? Were you two close?"

"Not as close as she was with your mother, of course, but close enough. I'm so devastated by her passing." Donna lowered her head and placed a hand over her heart.

Ellie took in the grieving friend image Donna presented. Perfect and poised, but faker than a knockoff Louis Vuitton. "Is that why you offered the reward?"

"Yes, and I actually just spoke with your lead detective. You guys are doing some amazing work. I'm told we've gotten great results from the tip line." The eyebrow Donna raised was smug, like her money would catch Monique's killer faster than the detectives working the case.

Great results?

Ellie doubted any of the tips the precinct received would be helpful. They'd only muddy the waters of an already murky case. "How long were you at the party that night?"

"All night. I'm a bit of a social butterfly."

Interesting.

When she and Lancaster reviewed the footage, Donna was absent for a good chunk of time that evening. "And you never left the party? Because there's a long stretch of security footage where you're missing."

Donna cleared her throat and averted her eyes. "I said I was there all night. The crab cakes were to die for." She chuckled.

Ellie cringed at the horrid pun. *Did she mean to make such an insensitive joke?* She pursed her lips. "What about Quint? The guy who just left the office."

"Quint Bannister?" Donna scoffed. "He's a friend. Nothing else."

A lie.

Ellie could tell by the way Donna's arms crossed, the way the stilted words sounded rehearsed, and the way her head bobbed up and down instead of left to right. *So Dan was right about the boyfriend.* "Was he at the event?"

"Not that I know of." Irritation crept into Donna's voice. "Does it matter?" She glanced at the clock on the wall.

"Is he a friend of your husband's as well?"

The older woman rose, her arms balancing her frame against the desk. "That's none of your damn business. Are we done here?"

Ellie stood and hiked the strap of her bag over her shoulder. "One more question. Why are you offering a reward to catch Monique's killer? What's in it for you?"

Donna laughed. "Seriously? When one of Charleston's elite suffers, we all suffer. You should know that, Detective Kline. Why, we've suffered enough because of you."

Ellie steadied her expression, unwilling to reveal her confusion to Donna. "What does that mean?"

One suffers, we all suffer. Wait, isn't that from one of the Corinthians?

The sneer on Donna's face reminded Ellie of a cornered animal, ready to attack. "We all talk about your kidnapping, your fantastical police pursuits. About how your actions make us all look bad. Thank heavens for your parents. They counteract all the negativity you bring to our society."

Oh. Like everything else for people like Donna, this is all about appearances and maintaining power. Donna didn't care about Monique's death at all.

Ellie refused the bait. Managing a sympathetic smile, she

relaxed her shoulders. "Actually, I don't think you need my help for that. You and your elites bring enough bitterness and bad energy to the table already."

Donna's cheeks flushed crimson. She slammed her butt back into her chair and yanked her laptop in front of her. "Is that all? I'm sure my receptionist mentioned I'm quite busy."

"Yes. Thank you for your time." Ellie spun around and swung the door to the lobby open, almost bumping smack dab into Quint.

Was he lingering out here and listening the whole time?

He lifted an eyebrow and puckered his lips. The smell of onions and potato chips swarmed her.

Fighting the urge to vomit, Ellie pushed past him and stalked through the lobby.

14

Fluorescent light on the ceiling buzzed, breaking the silence in the precinct conference room. Ellie dropped the banker's box onto the table with a *thud*, cringing as the overworked air conditioner squealed beside her.

After the interview with Donna, she needed to blow off steam. Donna hadn't lied about her being a troublemaker in the society circles. Still, she didn't appreciate the other woman attacking her by pointing out her rebellious nature.

Because work distracted Ellie best, she went straight from Broadside Insurance Company back to the police department and down to the basement, resuming her search for the archive files associated with the LaPierre Foundation. Half an hour later, after unboxing and re-boxing a dozen cardboard containers, she hit pay dirt. The cold case linked to the nonprofit.

Lancaster glanced up from the end of the table while Ellie removed the box's lid. "Employee interviews were a bust. I spoke to every staff member at the Coastline Inn, and no one remembers a dang thing that's useful."

She riffled through file folders. "What about the White

Gloves Catering folks? Have you gotten all the way through that list?"

"Yeah. I mean, I spoke with the manager, and he confirmed where everyone was that night."

"Did anyone report any food allergies or conflicts with the guests to the manager?" Dan was right about Donna. So maybe what he'd seen on his way to the restroom was also good information. If Monique had gotten the server dismissed that night, the manager would know.

"Food allergies? Uh, no. The guy in charge wasn't aware of anything weird happening that night. I did get this tidbit from him, though. White Gloves works very closely with the LaPierre Foundation. Most of the charity's graduates get hired by the catering company. That's why so many of the employees on our list had trouble in their backgrounds."

Ellie retrieved a file folder from the box and plopped into a chair. "That's one mystery solved." She stared at Lancaster and debated if she wanted to share the other information she'd learned. *Probably should. Us being partners and all.* "I spoke with my brother. Dan Kline. He's on your list."

If Lancaster was shocked by the revelation, he didn't show any surprise. He put down the paper he'd been studying and returned her stare.

"Dan thought he saw Monique arguing with a server. No one else saw the incident, though, and Dan said he was pretty drunk, so he may not have seen what he thought."

"That's not very reliable intel." Lancaster exhaled and went back to reading his paper.

Ellie bristled at her partner's lack of interest. While not much to go on, Dan's information was still a viable lead. "I have something else. I spoke to Donna Montague earlier."

He snorted. "The woman who went on television and offered the reward?"

"Yes. She's shallow and a showboater, but I don't think

she has any motive. She's just using Monique's death to grab a few seconds in the spotlight."

"So another dead end. Jeez. You'd think by now we'd have caught *some* sort of break." He rubbed his eyes.

Ellie raised a finger. "Maybe not a dead end completely. She has this assistant I think we should look at. Quint Bannister. Can you get a background check going for him?"

"Yeah, yeah." Lancaster gripped his pencil. "Q-u-i-n-t B-a-n-n-i-s-t-e-r, right?"

Ellie nodded before thumbing through the file folder she'd pulled from the box. She had one more lead to share. "And there's this...come take a look."

He walked around the conference table and leaned over her shoulder. "What've you got?"

She spread the papers out on the table. "This is a missing persons case from several years ago. The person was one of the kids helped by the LaPierre Foundation."

"That's interesting. They never found him, huh?" Lancaster sucked air through his teeth and shook his head. "But this could just be a coincidence. Kids go missing all over Charleston. Figures one of them could be from LaPierre."

"Except..." Ellie pulled a second file from the box, "there was another kid who went missing from LaPierre. These two cases were filed together. I'd poked around in this box when I worked cold cases, but I never got a chance to review the files before I was called up to homicide. These cases were buried together in the archives. Someone wanted to hinder anyone from performing the necessary due diligence to try and solve them."

Lancaster returned to his chair. "It's still coincidental. All we've got at the moment are rumors and speculation. No one's been able to prove or confirm anything. We've got bunk."

"But these cases were buried. Someone didn't want these

kids found. My guess is a person with high-level political contacts surrounding LaPierre."

Ellie scoured the documents, searching for some clue she was on the right track. Two kids associated with a charity had disappeared, and everyone looked the other way. Why?

"So what? Now we're considering conspiracy theories? C'mon. We deal with facts, not nonsense." Lancaster shook his head, clearly not buying the notion of something deeper going on. "The idea that the Powers That Be covered up for the LaPierre Foundation won't fly with no evidence."

Using her nail, she folded the corner of the file folder, wishing someone would listen to her for once. "It wouldn't be the first time a detective took a deal to spare some powerful person jail time."

Lancaster grunted. "I'm well aware our precinct has had its share of bad cops. I listen to the gossip too. But until you have more concrete evidence to support this theory, I'm focusing on facts. Beyond the apparently rogue security guard who tampered with the cameras, there's no reason to waste more of our attention on the staff at the hotel or the catering people. I say we look more closely at the guests."

Should we?

Ellie wasn't ready to take her attention off the employees. How in-depth had Lancaster's interviews been? He'd conducted all of them without her. Who knew if he asked the right questions?

She'd be happy when she didn't have to rely on a partner anymore. Although, she did appreciate when Lancaster took care of the little things like getting warrants and culling down the list of suspects.

Still, he moved fast, like he was trying to get a collar before the weekend. Ellie guessed Stoddard setting a priority status on catching Monique's killer prompted his hurry. The department heads wanted to tie the case up as soon as possible, but speed came at a price. Had some clue slipped through the cracks because of the expedited timeline?

Ellie massaged her throbbing temples.

Maybe the medical examiner could shed some light on this mess. Two bodies waited in the morgue. Surely, one of them could provide Ellie with useful information about the killer.

Tomorrow, she'd pay the M.E. a visit.

15

As birds flitted around the treetops, settling in for the evening, Ellie studied Bethany where the child held court on the balcony deck of their apartment. The change of scenery, from eating at the dining table inside to chowing down at the wrought iron bistro table outside, put a smile on the girl's face that Ellie hoped she'd never lose.

Jillian, Ellie's roommate, grinned. Her straight blond hair was swirled up into a messy bun. Scooching back, she leaned in close to Bethany, her chair legs scraping the concrete as she shifted. "Careful. Put too much in there and your words will get sticky."

"Really?" Bethany stopped chewing her peanut butter and jelly sandwich and turned to Jacob Garcia, Jillian's boyfriend and Ellie's former unit partner from her days as a patrol officer. Thanks to his ongoing relationship with her best friend, they'd stayed in contact since her promotion to homicide detective.

With Bethany in the other chair, he was the odd man out at the tiny table. Jacob shifted on the footstool Ellie found for him in a closet, his thick biceps flexing when he bit into his turkey sandwich. Mustard outlined the corners of his mouth as he winked at Bethany. "I think she's pulling your leg."

Bethany's smile returned, and she resumed chewing. Peering up at the brightening stars against the faded blue-and-pink sky, she sighed in contentment.

Ellie sensed a presence from behind only seconds before strong arms encircled her. "Sorry I'm late," Clay murmured, planting a kiss on her cheek.

She pressed her head back into the warmth of his stomach. "You missed the sandwiches. Want me to see what I can drum up in the kitchen?"

With a playful tug, he helped her to her feet, causing her to stumble into him. "A beer would be great. And I am a little peckish."

Two minutes later, Clay had his beer while Ellie dug around in the kitchen, trying to find him a snack. Animal crackers were vetoed as too sugary, pretzels as too salty, and their other options were limited. Groceries wouldn't be delivered until Saturday, and Ellie's cupboards were running dry.

Finally, he accepted her offer of guacamole and chips. Ellie tossed him a bag before heading for the fridge. She opened a clear drawer and rummaged through packages of cheese and yogurt, looking for the guac. Lifting a yogurt container, she glanced at the expiration date.

I really should clean out the fridge.

"Do y'all eat out there often?" Clay popped the top of his beer and dug into the tortilla chips.

"We didn't used to." She shoved a jar of sweet gherkins to the side. "When we were on vacation, Bethany told Mom she prefers wide-open spaces."

Clay sipped his beer. "That because of Kingsley?"

"He did kidnap Beth and keep her locked in a refrigerator as punishment for disobeying him." Ellie retrieved a bottle of mustard from the back of the shelf and stared at the inside of the appliance. Even if she removed the shelves and crusty drawer, there still wasn't much room. How had Bethany survived those hours and hours of torment?

A weight settled onto Ellie's shoulders. Her heartbeat sped up. It usually did when she allowed her thoughts to drift to the dark places Kingsley's memory still inhabited. Closing her eyes, she practiced the trick her therapist taught her. Air pushed into her lungs. She held it. *Six, five, four, three, two, one.* Ellie exhaled. *Six, five, four, three, two, one.*

"Ellie?" Concern pitched Clay's voice.

"Found it!"

She shut the refrigerator door and handed him a half-eaten container of guacamole. "Sorry, zoned out for a second. I think Bethany spent so much time confined that she gets edgy if trapped inside too long. Therapy has really helped her open up about what makes her happy and what doesn't. And I have no issue giving her as much outside time as she wants. I've even been looking at some of the hiking paths on James Island. You interested? We could make a weekend getaway of it, the three of us."

"Yeah, that sounds great." He dipped a chip into the guac and crunched it between his teeth.

Ellie handed him a napkin. "Guacamole and beer isn't a great dinner."

"It's fine. I had a big lunch with a buddy of mine. Ended up getting a full spread of steak, potatoes, rolls, and sweet tea." Clay patted his abs. "I'm still stuffed."

"Steak would be good right now. Better than the egg salad sandwich and chips I just ate."

Ellie ambled into the living room and collapsed on the couch. She glanced at the balcony deck, where Bethany ran in small circles. The dogs, Jillian's Sam and Jacob's Duke, chased after her, panting and barking and catching her quickly in the restrictive space.

Bethany would only get bigger from here. She deserved a huge yard for playing and daydreaming and running around.

Ellie's mind drifted to the tire swing still hanging from an old oak tree on her parents' property. As kids, she and her brother, Wesley, spent many hours pushing each other on that rubber doughnut. They'd also wiled away the lazy summer days reading comic books under the shade of the tree's sprawling branches and lush leaves.

I want Bethany to have nostalgic moments to remember when she's older too. She had experienced so much trauma in her life. The weight on Ellie's shoulders grew heavier, urging her to blast all of Bethany's terrible memories out of existence and replace them with new, happy ones.

"Clay, do you think it's time for me to find a different place to live? Someplace with more room for Bethany and maybe a yard she could play in?"

Without a word, Clay put the lid back on the guacamole dip and grabbed his beer. As he sat next to her on the couch, he scraped his thumbnail over the rim of the bottle. "Are you suggesting we buy a house? Me and you? I mean, the idea has crossed my mind. It would be good for Bethany, for sure. And me. And you. So I guess my answer is…yes."

Ellie twisted in his direction, struggling to hide her bemused expression at the way his voice cracked on the word *yes*.

"Those are just my thoughts, though. You're a strong and independent woman. I know you'll make the right decision for you and Bethany." Clay ran his free hand over the back of his neck, making him appear both adorable and vulnerable. "Plus, living in the tiny apartment they gave me in the FBI building is getting old. Why do you think I spend so much time over here?"

"It's good to know your thoughts." Ellie stifled a chuckle. The bumbling way the usually suave FBI agent answered her question lightened her spirit. "I'll start looking around. Who knows? Maybe I'll find the perfect place. For all of us."

Clay blushed before clearing his throat. "What about your case? Any progress?"

"I'm chipping away." Ellie exhaled and rested her head against the back of the couch cushion. "I've dug into the LaPierre Foundation a bit more. Not much has come up yet, but I'm getting there. There's a motive in the case somewhere. I'll figure out what it is, slowly but surely."

Clay picked at the label on his bottle. "You should know, the FBI's been investigating child trafficking and child abuse within the LaPierre system. The records are sealed because of the victims' ages, so all we have are rumors. I'm having trouble getting anything concrete."

"What?" The two missing-kid cases popped into Ellie's mind. "I've got a couple of cold cases where kids went missing while in LaPierre's care."

"Yeah, I've perused those files, too, on one of my visits to the precinct, but the details were flimsy at best. We think the trafficking ring involved LaPierre and a business named Delecroix Logistics. I've looked into them." Clay sipped more of his beer. "Haven't gotten far, though. They're protected by layers and layers of political red tape and creative financing."

Ellie straightened her back. Delecroix Logistics? Where had she heard that name before?

"I'm hoping this mess with Monique LaPierre's death is the event that unravels all of Delecroix's carefully structured barriers. That's my long-winded way of saying you should let me know if you need any help."

"I will. Thanks."

Clay smiled.

The screen door to the balcony slid open with a loud

bang. Bethany and Sam burst inside. Duke raced in behind them.

Bethany held a dirty plate in the air and ran to the kitchen, giggling as both dogs jumped to lick the remaining peanut butter. Her shrill voice enveloped the room. "No. No, doggies, no."

In the commotion, Jacob appeared at the screen door and whistled at the canines. Both whirled around and galloped back outside. He slid the screen door shut again.

"Whew." Bethany brushed her forehead in an exaggerated motion. "I didn't think I was going to make it."

Ellie laughed and shifted closer to the edge of the couch. "Go rinse your dish and start getting ready for bed, okay? It's getting late, and you have school tomorrow."

Bethany skipped over to the sink. Porcelain clattered against metal, and water burst from the faucet. The little girl returned to the living room and barreled into Ellie, looping her arms around her neck. "Thank you for letting me eat outside."

"Anytime. Sometimes you've got to get out and get some fresh air. I know what being cooped up feels like." Ellie blinked back tears. "You know you have me as a partner, right? Not just a parent. It's you and me against the world, and the only way we're going to win is if we work together."

"I know." Bethany loosened her grip with a smile. "Okay, good night."

She disappeared down the hall.

Clay reached over to lace his fingers through Ellie's. "You've got a really great connection with Bethany, you know that?"

Do I? She shook her head, casting the question away. *Be positive.* "I have to admit, things are going pretty well. All things considered."

But for how long?

That nagging voice in the back of her brain piped up again. Over the years, Ellie had learned one truth. Things never stayed the same. Bad things got good, and good things got bad.

How long until this one turns bad?

16

Nightclubs were not my thing any more than Italian cuisine was.

I lingered across the street from Retro, a downtown club. Neon lights flashed the name into the night. The rhythmic thump of the music from inside, each beat a soul-crushing scream, echoed into the streets. I reconsidered the whole damn plan and turned, ready to leave the noise and commotion behind.

Remember the goal. Two birds. One stone.

Spinning back around, I steeled my resolve, conjuring the image of Dan Kline and the detective eating high on the hog at Rosarito's. Which was good. It was Dan's last meal, after all. My fingertips caressed the packet of powder in my pocket.

Thanks to my eavesdropping, I knew Dan recalled seeing me with Monique the night she died. And that he and the detective were related, meaning grief over his death would stall her investigation.

I stepped onto the street, then hopped back onto the curb. *Do I have to take care of him here?* Nightclubs brought out the worst in me. Triggers lurked behind the purple metal door across the street. Triggers I might not be able to handle.

It has to be now. Before Dan remembers anything else about that night.

Dodging cars, I darted across the road before I could change my mind again. An old buddy guarded the entrance.

As I approached, Mike uncrossed his brawny arms. "Hey, man. Haven't seen you in a while. Looking good." He gave me a thumbs-up.

"Thanks, man." I leaned in. "Listen, my girl wanted me to meet her an hour ago. I'm really late, and she's probably pissed. By the time I get through this line, she'll be my ex-girlfriend. Think you can help me out?"

"Aw, man. You know I got your back. Go on." My buddy shuffled to the side, giving me space to scoot by behind him.

Yelps and groans erupted from the queued people, but I didn't give a shit. They were Mike's problem. I smirked as I whizzed by them and entered the club.

Sweaty people grinding and gyrating against each other packed the floor. My stomach knotted. *Will I even be able to find Danny boy in all this chaos? Also, do none of these people have to work in the morning?*

When the song changed, a roar broke out around the club. Pulsating beats thumped in my head like a hangover from hell. A chick with curly blond hair crashed into my shoulder, screaming, *"This is my jam."*

The smell of hairspray and alcohol, swirled with nicotine and sweat, turned my stomach. I yanked at my shirt collar, trying to free myself from the heat and beats slamming against my body.

Squinting into the darkness, I studied the moving mass of damp skin. *Where are you, Danny boy?* As if on cue, the crowd parted, and I caught a glimpse of him several feet in front of me.

Got you.

He swayed at a table littered with empty beer mugs. A blue t-shirt and dark jeans replaced the suit he'd worn earlier in the day. He was alone but scanning the crowd intently, probably searching for his friends or a hot chick to take home.

If only, pretty boy.

I ducked to avoid detection, my back crashing into a table and splashing a guy's drink on his shoes. After glancing down at the mess, he glared. "Real smooth, asshole. Watch where you're going."

Resisting the urge to punch his stupid, ugly-ass face, I gritted my teeth and forced myself to stay focused. *Blend in and quit drawing attention.*

I retreated into the sea of bodies, waiting for the moment to strike.

Spit pooled in the back of my throat when arms and hands started flying at me from every direction. "Stop touching me."

The music drowned out my words. I clasped my ears as the pulsating beat continued to pound my chest like a bass drum.

Every person in sight was rich. I hated them, with their easy laughs and lies and lives. Without money, none of them would get a second glance on the street. The difference between them and me? I struggled every damn day of my life while they carried buckets of cash to throw at whatever they desired.

A woman to my left shrieked into my ear, her shrill laughter practically blowing out my eardrum. Another person knocked me to the side. My chest tightened, and a bolt of panic streaked through me. As all the air in the club vanished, I gasped for breath.

These aren't people. These are monsters in human form. Like the jerks who promised to help me. Instead, they helped themselves *to* me. To my body. They hurt me, and no one cared.

A hand slapped against my arm. I whirled around to punch the person, but there were so many faces. Laughing at me. Screaming at me.

My cheeks burned like waves of molten lava.

They knew. They knew all about what happened to me and didn't give a shit. No, not as long as their precious money was safe. They didn't care how they made their money either. These fuckers didn't have a damn worry in the world. Wads of cash plugged their ears while they chanted, *lalala, I can't hear you.*

I blindly groped for a wall, untangling appendages and kicking feet until I reached a corner. Pressing my cheek against the hard, cool surface, I rested against the wall and talked myself off the ledge. *Breathe. Get a fucking grip.*

Dan stepped away from the table.

I closed my eyes. *Come on, you asshole. Get it together, or you'll miss your chance.* I clenched my fist until it ached, replacing rage with pain. My cheeks cooled, and the pressure in my chest abated.

When I opened my eyes, Dan was waving at his buddies and wandering over to the stage, where the live band was setting up for their show. He motioned to the drummer, who ducked down and nodded.

My breathing calmed. *Dan's distracted. This is my chance.* As I elbowed through the crowd toward the table, I made a few extra hard jabs at random body parts.

The handle on Dan's mug was chipped. I hovered over the beer, pinching the package in my pocket. *This is his glass, right?* I eyed the other mugs. The glass in front of me was nearest to Dan's seat.

Being as discreet as possible, I whipped out the package

and sprinkled crushed powder into Dan's flattening beer. Without breaking stride, I sauntered over to the bar and bought myself a cold one. The beer flowed down my throat, nice and easy. I sipped slowly and monitored my target.

He returned to the table with his friends, cracking a joke that sent the whole group into guffaws. I licked my lips in anticipation as Dan reclaimed his seat and lifted the glass I'd doctored. He glugged the beverage down, his Adam's apple bobbing with each gulp.

My body sagged in relief. *Mission accomplished. Neither Kline will bother me anymore.* For once, like people with money, I would have my cake and eat it too. And the icing on that cake?

Tonight, at least one of those rich pukes would get what they deserved.

17

Bethany's tennis shoes scraped on the sidewalk leading into her school as she skipped along, swinging Ellie's hand back and forth with her own and humming a bouncy tune.

"You're extra chipper this morning." Excitement buzzed in the air. Children jumped and yelled in the courtyard while their parents wrangled them toward the front doors.

Bethany grinned. "Yep! Lyndy said she has a present for me."

"Oh? So today's an extra special day."

Ellie took a deep breath, inhaling the sweet, earthy scent of fresh cut grass.

"It is, but sad too. Lyndy and her family are going to Italy next month, so I won't see her at all during the summer." Bethany gazed up at Ellie with wide dark-brown eyes. "What if she makes new friends and doesn't want to be mine anymore when school starts again?"

Ellie knelt to meet Bethany's gaze, offering a comforting smile. "True friends always find their way back to each other, no matter how far they travel or how many new friends they make. Maybe you and Lyndy can write to each other over the summer. Share your adventures. It can be a fun way to keep your friendship strong."

Bethany's face brightened at the idea. "That's a really good idea. Maybe we can buy her some paper and a pen?"

"That's a really good idea too." Ellie stood, gently ruffling her hair. "And speaking of adventures, what would you like to do this summer?"

"I want to go swimming, and to the movies, and to visit Caraleigh and Luke, and…" Bethany counted down on her fingers as she listed items off.

Ellie half listened. She still hadn't decided on what to do with Bethany for the summer. The child needed care during the day, and Ellie didn't want to depend on her parents to babysit for the entire break.

Maybe I could find a fun day camp, or send Bethany to a full-on summer camp?

Bethany was still listing off items when they reached the school entrance.

Ellie knelt down to straighten the straps of the little girl's backpack. "I tell you what, you sit down tonight and write out everything you want to do this summer. Then we'll start making plans. Deal?" She held out a pinky.

The little girl hooked her pinky around Ellie's. "Deal."

Ellie waited for Bethany's pink backpack to disappear into the crowd before heading back to her SUV. Time was getting away from her. She needed to figure out what to do with Bethany for the next couple of months, and soon.

❄

When she arrived at the precinct, Lancaster was already in the conference room reviewing files. He'd obtained a warrant for copies of the LaPierre Foundation's financial records, which was a relief. After grabbing a coffee from the kitchen, she joined him.

"What are we looking for?" Lancaster lifted his water bottle to his lips.

"Connections. Any accounting transactions referencing Delecroix Logistics." Ellie settled into a seat near the door before pulling a pile of papers toward her.

"Why Delecroix? What do they have to do with LaPierre? I thought we were just going to look into the financials for discrepancies. Not something specific."

Ellie sipped her coffee as she considered how much to tell him. "I have a hunch. I got a tip that Delecroix and LaPierre could be linked in some shady practices. So look for discrepancies and any mentions of Delecroix."

A half hour later, they'd scoured through most of the documents and come up empty. Ellie released a frustrated sigh. *There's nothing? Really?*

She switched over to the secure email app on her laptop. Maybe the change of technological scenery would yield results. Once she signed on, a new message notification popped onto the screen. The background check on Quint Bannister confirmed he'd been in plenty of trouble with the law before.

Is it possible he, like Greg Chavin, worked with White Gloves Catering? Donna was evasive when Ellie pressed her for information on whether Quint was at the party. Maybe because he was staff.

Reaching across the table, Ellie grabbed the staff list Lancaster had created. Her finger trailed down the page, halting midway. "Gregory Chavin's name is crossed off. Did you talk to him already?"

"I did. Over the phone. I also spoke with his boss, who corroborated that Chavin punched out thirty minutes before

Monique went upstairs." Lancaster flipped a paper over and made a few marks on the page.

"What about those poker buddies he mentioned? We should talk to them too."

"Already ahead of you." He shoved the paper aside and grabbed another from his pile. "Chavin provided me with a list of their names, and I gave each one a call. They all verified his alibi."

"You said he punched out at what time?" She fumbled under her own pile of paperwork, hunting for the thumb drive with the security footage.

Lancaster balanced his elbow on the table, resting his head on his fist. "Eight."

Ellie plugged in the drive. "Do you want to come view this footage with me? It'll give you something besides dead trees to look at."

He stretched his arms before rising from his chair. "Sure. Legs could use a bit of movement anyway." He meandered toward Ellie and bent over her shoulder.

Together, they stared at the screen. Ellie dragged her fingertip across the touchpad, fast-forwarding the video to right before eight p.m. None of the footage included Monique. Could that have been during her intense conversation with the server? If her brother's information was reliable, it was possible. Ellie chewed on her nail.

"Next person on the list to be interviewed is Kira Long." Lancaster's voice was low and deep in her ear. "She's the director of the LaPierre Foundation. I'm already up, and I'm guessing both of us could use a break from these pages. Think we should head on over?"

He was right. Ellie could use a breather. Searching for the footage of Monique and the server could wait until later. She closed her laptop.

"Thought you'd never ask."

18

The building housing the LaPierre Foundation loomed before Ellie. Rising roughly a hundred feet toward the sky, the structure screamed elegance and influence. Rusticated bricks in gray and lighter gray scaled the walls. Arched windows, divided into fourteen panes, reflected the morning light. Thick columns of marbled white-and-gold stone stretched across the center. The clean, symmetrical architecture evoked images of the Parthenon.

Lancaster released a low whistle. "Man, this place is fancy for a nonprofit agency. I'd expected something less upscale."

"Like what?" Ellie climbed the smooth steps leading to the building.

"I don't know. Something located closer to the people being helped, I guess. Maybe in North Charleston." He trudged up the stairs behind her.

She let the comment sit. The LaPierre Foundation helped kids. *Does their location really matter?*

Still, she couldn't argue with his logic. Charleston was a big place. Satellite offices in the recipients' neighborhoods would make sense. At least more sense than this logistical nightmare that required those in need to travel, often under challenging circumstances, to receive assistance.

Rounding the top of the steps, Ellie pulled one of the two glass doors wide open and grinned at Lancaster. "Age before beauty."

He frowned, muttering something she couldn't quite catch as he continued inside.

The lobby was less impressive than the exterior. Shiny stone tiles spread across the floor, all of them white except for a set of blue ones in the middle. The tiles led from the front entrance to a reception desk, where a diminutive woman in cat-eye glasses stared at a computer screen. An oversize painting of blue-and-yellow abstract art decorated the wall behind her.

Ellie and Lancaster followed the path to the reception desk.

"Good morning. We'd like to speak with Kira Long." Lancaster towered over the woman, whose name tag read, *Himari*.

Raising a slim finger, Himari shoved the bridge of her glasses higher onto her nose. Her eyes remained glued to the screen while she typed on her keyboard. "Do you have an appointment?"

"No." Ellie leaned against the desk and held out her badge. "But we were hoping she'd make some time in her schedule for us anyway."

Himari sighed. Annoyance flickered across her face, but she quickly replaced the indiscretion with a polite smile. As she tilted her head, her long strands of jet-black hair fell to one side. "Of course. Please take a seat over there. I'll notify Ms. Long that you're here."

She gestured to a waiting area behind the detectives and picked up the receiver of a beige phone.

Ellie and Lancaster ambled to a set of blue-striped

couches and chairs near a window. A hall with a bank of elevators separated the space from the reception desk. Lancaster eased into a chair and pulled out his phone.

Is this the typical experience for anyone who comes to the LaPierre Foundation for help?

Ellie stepped toward the window behind Lancaster's seat and gazed out. A man in a faded t-shirt and work boots passed by on a bicycle. Across the street, a gaggle of young girls stumbled out of a dress boutique, shopping bag handles strung along their arms like rings above a shower curtain.

While the foundation's location on Market Street was in a good cross section of Charleston, the attitude inside the building projected a very South of Broad vibe. Not snobby, but exclusive. Selective. Ellie scrutinized the lobby's cold white walls and dim track lighting along the ceiling. No part of the decor was welcoming.

"Detectives?"

Ellie and Lancaster turned their heads toward a tall woman in a tailored mint-green brocade suit, her long brown hair curling around her shoulders. The heels of her gold stilettos *clinked* across the hard floor. She held out a hand. "I'm Kira Long."

They each shook Kira's hand before following her to her office and settling into a pair of comfy armchairs in front of her desk. Both Lancaster and Ellie declined the offer of tea or coffee. They were here for answers, not niceties paid for by well-meaning donations.

Ellie dove in headfirst. "What do you do for the foundation, Ms. Long?"

The woman shot them a toothy grin. "What do I not do? Seriously, though, I'm pretty much the heart of this place. Monique was the owner and chief financial supplier of the nonprofit, but I'm the director. I run the day-to-day operations."

Lancaster shifted in his seat. "How long had you and Mrs. LaPierre worked together?"

"About ten years or so. Technically, I worked for her husband until his death, but Monique and I knew each other." Kira batted her eyelashes, her smile faltering. "It's awful, really. First Hal, and now Monique. I suppose I'll be working with Jackie once the paperwork clears."

Ellie scrutinized the woman's sleek clothing and ritzy style. Not the type of person she'd pictured running the LaPierre Foundation. "Pardon the assumption, but you seem awfully young for this job."

Kira squared her shoulders. "Not at all. Hard work and dedication, those will take you everywhere. But I get that a lot. I'm forty-one, in case you were wondering."

The sound of laughter drifted from the hallway. Ellie clocked the expensive trinkets decorating Kira's desk and walls. Framed art, most likely originals. A gold-plated stapler. Leather chairs. A diamond-encrusted calculator. *Who would've guessed that even math can be fancy?* This was the extravagance she'd expected to find in Donna Montague's office, not a charity director's.

"What exactly does the foundation do? You work with kids, right?" The air conditioning clicked on, freezing Ellie within seconds. She glanced up. *Right under the vent. Perfect.*

"Young people. Kids, teenagers, that age. We help troubled youth move past their juvenile offenses and inspire them to embark on a fresh start. Our connections are with foster services and companies willing to help out. Get them jobs. Housing. That sort of thing." Kira folded her hands on top of her desk and beamed.

Lancaster clicked his tongue. "Not all criminals can be redeemed, and some of your recipients have had very disturbing records. How do you ensure they're truly on the straight and narrow?"

Ellie piggybacked on Lancaster's query. "Like Lou Cramer. He works for White Gloves Catering." *And has a criminal record longer than my inseam.*

"It's possible he's one of ours. We work tightly with White Gloves Catering. Our job is to help people lead normal lives." Kira cleared her throat and leveled her gaze. "Of course, that's not really possible if the police are jumping to conclusions about our beneficiaries every time something bad happens."

Ellie reared back, ready to strike. "Are there any specific former charity recipients who could be capable of killing Monique? Anyone with a grudge?"

She stopped short of asking Kira about the rumors of a trafficking ring using kids in LaPierre's recipient pool. That was Clay's case, not hers.

"I'm sorry?" Kira frowned and raised her chin. "These are troubled kids, not murderers."

Lancaster shrugged. "All murderers were kids once. Gotta start somewhere."

"That doesn't mean any of *our* kids are murderers. The implication is grotesque." Kira wrinkled her nose in disgust.

"It is." Lancaster spread his hands. "That's why we'd like to look at your records. That way, we can rule out any of the LaPierre Foundation's recipients."

Ellie's gaze flitted to the file cabinet behind Kira. On the top, silver-and-gold frames displayed photos of Kira socializing with Charleston's elite.

Kira shook her head. "Nope. Not without a warrant. Our beneficiaries are juveniles. Their records are protected."

Softening her voice, Ellie approached the conversation from a different angle. "I understand, but those files could help us catch Monique's killer. There's no way we can get a peek?"

She suspected the answer wouldn't change. Kira gave off stickler-for-rules vibes. They *were* talking about her foundation's murdered benefactor, though. Perhaps reminding Kira of that fact could sway her.

"No. Not going to happen." Kira furrowed her brows and stood, her lips tightening into a thin line. "Let me show you out."

"All right." Ellie nodded and rose, along with Lancaster. "We'll be back soon. With a warrant."

Outside, Lancaster whistled again as they descended the slick stairs in front of the foundation. "She's a tough nut to crack."

Ellie shrugged while basking in the sun's warmth. After sitting under Kira's arctic air vent, the heat on her skin was therapeutic. "Can't begrudge her for refusing to break the rules. Would've made our job a little easier, though."

"Once we get back to the station, I'll start preparing the paperwork for the warrant." He retrieved his keys from his pocket.

"Sounds good. And while we're waiting—" A buzz in Ellie's pocket startled her. She held up a finger and mouthed, *hold on.* "Hello?"

"Ellie? Oh, god, Ellie, you've got to get to the hospital, please. It's Dan." Her mom broke into a sob.

"What? Dad?"

His heart. Oh, god. It's finally happening. He's taking a turn for the worse.

"No, no. Your brother." A shaky breath escaped from the other end of the line. "He's been rushed to the university medical center. He was convulsing and violently ill when they found him. Please, you have to get here."

"On my way." Ellie ended the call and pressed her hand against her chest, desperate to slam the brakes on her speeding heartbeat. *Dan? Convulsing and violently ill? What the hell happened?*

She shoved her phone back into her pocket and pointed at a confused Lancaster as she raced back to her SUV.

"See if we have enough for a warrant. I've got to get to the hospital. Something's wrong with my brother."

19

Ellie burst out of the elevator and rushed to the hospital waiting room, scanning the crowded area for her parents. The stench of bleach in the stale air burned her nose.

"Princess. Over here."

Her parents sat in two chairs bordering a white wall in the corner. A square table with scattered magazines and pamphlets separated them from a wide-eyed woman holding a toddler with a bloody finger. Ellie's father ran his bony fingertips through his silver hair and glanced back at her mother. His pink polo shirt wrinkled across his thin torso with the movement.

Ellie stumbled forward and stood in front of them. She'd never seen her mother so pale and disheveled. While her words caught in the back of her throat, she managed to free a couple. "What happened?"

Helen's head sank as she clutched the arms of the chair. "We don't know…"

Dan patted his wife's arm before raising weary eyes to Ellie. "He went out last night. Had a few drinks. He claims he didn't eat anything unusual. Said the only odd thing about the evening was that his drink tasted funny. Skunked. That's the word he used. He said the beer bothered his stomach. Between that and staying out a little too late, he wasn't up to going into the office this morning, so he called in sick and slept in."

"His cleaning woman found him, thank god." Her mother's voice trembled. "He was convulsing on the floor when she got there."

A scratchy announcement for Doctor Lawson to get to the ER blared over the PA system. Ellie cringed at the abrasiveness.

"Luckily, she'd seen this before and knew to roll Dan over so he wouldn't choke on…" her father took a deep breath, "on his own vomit. She's also the one who called nine one one."

Ellie met with a joking, annoying, normal Dan yesterday. What happened between then and now?

The club. If I'd accepted his invitation to go to Retro, would he be okay?

A group of people on the other side of the room jumped up and surrounded a frail man in white. A woman in the group wailed and doubled over. Nausea rolled through Ellie's stomach, threatening to redirect all of the contents to her mouth. Dropping into the seat next to her mother, she struggled to slow her breathing.

Please, don't let that happen to Dan. Let him be okay.

"It was touch-and-go for a while, but Danny's doing okay. At the moment, at least. I mean, he's in a medically induced coma, but he's stable…" Helen's quiet sob spoke volumes.

Ellie threw her arms around her mother's shoulders. When tears sprouted in the corners of her eyes, she blinked them back. "Do they have any idea what's wrong? Did someone put a drug in his drink, or is this some kind of virus?"

"They aren't sure of much yet, but they've ruled out a viral infection." Her father clasped his hands and stared at them. A single tear trailed down his face, dripping off his chin. "It's possible he has a potential food allergy or alcohol poisoning. They haven't been able to isolate the specific cause, though. They're running more tests."

Her mother hugged herself and sank into the chair. "Why did this happen? Monique fell over a balcony and died. Now Danny's sick and in the hospital and…" She clamped her mouth shut.

"Will be fine," Ellie finished, somehow managing to keep her voice even.

"I feel like I did something wrong. Like I'm being punished." Helen's harsh whisper caught some people's attention.

Ignoring the stares, her father tut-tutted and gripped his wife's shoulders. The skin hung loose on his muscles. "Don't talk like that. Ellie's right. Dan will be fine. None of this is your fault."

Helen rested her head against his shoulder, her body melting into his.

Ellie checked her watch and tensed. Bethany. *Dammit.* She rose, her back and neck muscles tightening. Leaving now, when her parents and brother needed her? Guilt clogged her throat. "Mom, I'm so sorry to do this, but it's almost time to pick Beth up. I've got to get to the school."

Her mother sniffled before swiping her cheek with the back of her hand. "Call Greta. She'd probably be able to pick Bethany up and keep an eye on her for a while. And Blake is on his way. We'll be fine."

Ellie's shoulders relaxed. It would be best if Bethany wasn't forced to hang out with them at the hospital all night. "All right. I'll give her a call and get a coffee. Do you want anything? Water? Snacks?"

They both shook their heads. After giving her mother another hug, Ellie wandered into the hall and dialed the house phone number.

Greta picked up on the first ring. "Kline residence."

Ellie explained the dilemma to her parents' house manager, her voice cracking as she struggled with her emotions. She could cry later, after she made sure Beth was taken care of.

Greta didn't hesitate. "I'll leave right away. Louis can whip her up some dinner tonight. You stay there and take care of your folks. We've got everything under control here."

"Thank you." Ellie ended the call and slumped against the wall.

Her vision blurred. *Dan was so excited yesterday about his promotion. What if he doesn't make it?* She hurried to the nearest restroom and, once there, released all the pain swelling in her heart.

Five minutes later, she splashed cold water on her face and exhaled so deeply, her stomach flattened like a crepe. Her parents needed her, and she wouldn't help anyone by crying in a stall.

As she exited the restroom, she gazed at the vending machines and tried to decide whether a time like this called for more caffeine or less. Erring on the side of being less high-strung for the evening, she slipped a dollar into the machine for a bottle of water instead.

By the time she returned to the waiting room, her father was gone. She sat on the edge of the chair next to her mother. "Where's Dad?"

"He went to the bathroom." Her mother stared blankly into the open space between the nurse's desk and the rows of chairs in the waiting room. "Probably trying to track down the doctor for an update."

Ellie bit her lip. "This doesn't make sense. Why would someone try to hurt Dan?"

Does it have something to do with the party?

Her mother was right. Within seventy-two hours, Monique and the security guard had died, and Dan was in a medically induced coma.

Ellie didn't believe in coincidences. Not like these anyway.

Her mother's red-rimmed eyes remained vastly empty, like if she waited and stared hard enough, Dan would be saved. "I don't know, Eleanor. At this point, we're helpless. All we can do is pray and wait."

Ellie hated waiting games. The way her chest tightened in the mounting tension until she couldn't breathe. The tremble in her heart from not knowing how the game would end. It was pure torture.

She couldn't sit around and wait. Her brother needed her. If his mysterious illness was tied to what happened to Monique and Bernard, she didn't have time to hold back. The killer had a knack for making his murders look like accidents.

First, she needed to find the doctor and let him know about her suspicions. It might spark ideas for tests or treatments the medical team hadn't considered yet.

Dan Kline would not be lumped in with those "accidents." The best doctors in the state were taking care of him. He would recover.

And the monster doing all this?

You're mine.

20

Ellie pressed the buttons of the keypad leading into the morgue. A chirp sounded, and the doors *whooshed* open. As she stepped inside, the powerful odor of disinfectant and sanitizer hit her nose. Despite the attempt to cover up the smell, she still detected the underlying scent permeating every inch of the room.

Death.

Ellie donned a paper apron and snapped a pair of gloves onto her hands before slipping a pair of blue booties over her shoes. Doctor Moniza Faizal hovered over two tables when Ellie entered the autopsy room. The willowy medical examiner's thick black hair was fastened into a tight bun at the nape of her neck. A white lab coat was a lovely contrast to her brown skin.

Beside her, the bodies of Monique LaPierre and Bernard Cookson lay naked on the slabs, yellow tags attached to their toes. Bright LED tubes humming in the ceiling emitted a cold, harsh light over the bodies.

Ellie's booties *swish-swished* as she shuffled over to the M.E.

The doctor turned her head and grinned. "How have you been, Detective Kline? I heard you had an exciting vacation."

"The job never stops." Ellie shivered in the icy chill of the room.

"Shall we begin?" Doctor Faizal directed Ellie's attention to Monique's body. "I've been working diligently on both, but Bernard's not ready yet. I've just finished Monique's assessment, though."

Ellie crossed her arms. "Okay, what've we got?"

The doctor inhaled sharply, as if bracing herself. "Cause of death was blunt force trauma due to falling from a great height. In this case, onto the rocks. The victim suffered fractures to her skull and spine, as well as several lacerations to her upper back, the back of her head, and her limbs." She motioned toward the areas on Monique's arms.

"All consistent with a fall."

Ellie leaned in and studied the rips and scrapes on Monique's gray skin. An ugly blend of burgundy-and-black wounds and bruises were all that remained of the pain Monique endured after she hit the rocks.

"Yes, as is the ruptured spleen and collapsed lungs. These are all trademarks of a sudden impact from a fall. But…" Doctor Faizal stepped back and met Ellie's gaze. "The cause of death is only part of this poor woman's story."

Ellie tilted her head, curiosity edging into her brain. "That's not something I usually hear. What's special about Monique LaPierre's death?"

The M.E. returned her attention to the table. "The victim was in the early stages of pregnancy. That, by itself, is a tragic discovery to make while examining a corpse. Add in the fact that Monique LaPierre was fifty-two years old, her husband was dead, and we received no information regarding a boyfriend, and…well, I'm stunned."

The medical examiner wasn't the only one.

Pregnant?

That revelation transformed the entire investigation by bringing a new motive to the table. Money, revenge, and impending, unwanted fatherhood. *But who's the dad?* After her husband's death, Monique had spent the last two years on the social scene alone. Whoever she'd been seeing, she'd been doing so in hush-hush private.

"Can we get a DNA test on the fetus?" Ellie's gaze drifted to Monique's midsection.

"Sure." Doctor Faizal made a note on a clipboard hanging from the wall. "Just keep in mind, the results could be inconclusive. If the father's DNA isn't on file, matching him up to the unborn child might be impossible."

"I understand. I'll see about getting cheek swabs for everyone who attended the black-tie event that night. It'll need to be voluntary, but it'll give us a list for those who refuse. Maybe we'll luck out."

If the father was there, that might've been the catalyst for the murder.

Ellie continued to take shallow breaths until the door to the morgue shut behind her and fresh air from the hallway rushed into her lungs. Pulling her phone out of her pocket, she dialed Lancaster's number.

"You're not going to believe the autopsy report." Ellie filled him in on Doctor Faizal's findings.

On the other end of the line, Lancaster whistled low and loud. Ellie winced and held the device a couple inches away. She could picture him shaking his head. "Pregnant? Didn't see that one coming."

"You and me both." Ellie returned the phone to her ear. "Can you start making some calls? Let's try to get every male partygoer to give a cheek swab. We'll start things off on a voluntary basis."

"Will do. There's going to be a few hoity-toity partygoers

who aren't going to like what we're implying." Lancaster lowered his voice. "We can probably expect some irate calls to the captain."

The captain of the police department, Gil Browning, was known for his desire to climb Charleston's social ladder. Vain enough to dye his hair an unnatural shade of black long after he'd gone gray and adept enough to wiggle his way into many society galas, he was the first person any member of the elite would call if they had an issue with the cheek swabs.

"If anyone pushes back or refuses, we'll dig into them deeper and see if we can get enough probable cause to involve a judge and get some warrants lined up. Don't worry about Captain Browning, though." If necessary, Ellie could handle him. "For now, let's stay positive. Start with voluntary cheek swabs, and we'll see where that takes us."

❄

Ellie pressed the doorbell of the LaPierre mansion once and waited. After a few minutes, she pushed the button a second time. *Maybe Jackie isn't home and I can put this off a little longer.* She was about to head back toward her SUV when the jiggle of a lock caught her attention.

Jackie appeared in the doorway, holding a large glass of white wine. Her bloodshot eyes widened, deepening the dark circles beneath. "Oh, hi."

"Can I come in for a moment?"

Jackie's drained expression sliced through Ellie's heart, and a throbbing pain pounded between her ears. She was about to drop a bombshell on her old friend, and she wished to God she didn't have to.

Jackie swung the door open wider. "Absolutely. Care for a glass?" The stem in Jackie's hand wobbled between her fingers.

Ellie stepped into the foyer. "No, thank you. Jackie, I need to talk with you about something we've discovered in the investigation. Can we sit?"

The entire drive over, she'd imagined how she would take the same news. Jackie just lost her mother. Now she was about to find out she'd lost a sibling too. Ellie didn't relish being the one to cause such pain and confusion.

If I were in Jackie's place, I probably would be better off not even knowing the baby existed.

The story would get out, though. Gossip in Charleston spread faster than ivy on an iron gate.

Hearing the news from a friend would be better than picking up the truth from whispers in a restaurant restroom. Ellie had overheard plenty of stories about herself that way from women who didn't care that she was next to them, in a stall or even washing her hands. Rumors came with being the daughter of a wealthy socialite. They were nasty, but they were also a price to pay for wealth.

"Yeah, let's go out on the deck. I could use some fresh air."

Jackie shut the door and gestured to the left with her glass, leading Ellie through a maze of doorways and halls.

"Are you alone?" Ellie's voice echoed in the empty rooms as she trailed Jackie.

Her friend nodded. "I sent everyone away. The housekeeper, the chef, even Greg. I couldn't think straight with all of them hovering over me."

They passed through a sunroom with honey-colored wooden beams on the ceiling and metal chairs, painted a matching shade, on the floor. White cushions dotted the seats. A slate-blue table with an exquisite model ship on display sat between the chairs. Jackie unlocked a latch at the side of one of the tall windows surrounding the room and slid the glass to the side. She stepped out onto the deck before making her way to a flat-roof pergola near the edge of a covered swimming pool.

A symphony of crickets serenaded Ellie as she slipped through the door. Around the pergola, hanging rattan lanterns emitted a dim glow.

Ellie tapped one with her finger. "These are lovely." It was small talk. A feeble attempt to delay the conversation a second longer.

Jackie placed her wine glass on a teak side table and slumped onto a deck chair. "They're solar-powered. They'll get brighter as it gets darker."

"Cool." Ellie pointed to a fire pit several feet to the side of the pergola, off the deck. Stacked stones in deep reds and browns served as the foundation of the squarish structure. The top was a thick slab of white marble with gold flecks. "That's unique. Most of the ones I've seen are built with faded rocks."

"Dad built that. We haven't used the pit since he passed away. Mom didn't have the heart. She said the fire died with him." Jackie retrieved her wine and took a deep gulp before placing the glass back on the table. Her fingertips fidgeted with a lock of her dark hair. "So you said something about news?"

"Yeah." There was no easy way to reveal the information, so it was better to not hesitate any longer. "It's about your mom. I spoke to the medical examiner this afternoon, and…"

Jackie lowered her glistening eyes and tugged a little harder on her hair. "What? She had cancer or something?"

"No." Ellie bent forward and rested her palm on Jackie's knee. "She was pregnant."

The crickets' song seemed to reach a crescendo as Jackie stared at Ellie. After several long seconds, she guffawed. "No way. That's a lie."

Ellie drew her hand back and straightened. She'd

expected a worse reaction. Anger. Tears. It never occurred to her that Jackie would simply not believe her. "It's not. She was pregnant. Do you know if your mom was seeing anyone?"

"Hell no. Not after Dad died." Jackie leaned forward, her palm on her chest and her fingers splayed over her heart. "I don't think you understand. Dad was it for her. She wouldn't have even *looked* at anyone else, much less been intimate with them."

Ellie needed Jackie to accept the truth. "Your mom was pregnant."

"Stop saying that." She ran a clenched fist over her hair, her eyes darting from side to side. "There's no way. Why would she keep that from me? Pregnant?"

"She may not have known…"

Jackie grabbed her glass and gulped the rest of her wine. A moth flitted against a hanging lantern above them, jostling the burgeoning light in the darkening pergola. Jackie swallowed hard. "Can you go? I want to be alone."

"I don't know if you should be—"

"Leave, Ellie. Please." Jackie's hair draped over her face like a shroud, preventing Ellie from reading her expression.

She reached over and touched Jackie's arm. "If anyone comes to mind that you think could've been the father, let me know, okay?"

Jackie nodded. "Yeah. Of course. Let yourself out, all right?"

Driving down the LaPierre driveway in the dwindling darkness, unease settled over Ellie. *Somebody should be with Jackie right now.* Guilt crept into her chest, tightening her muscles until she struggled to breathe.

She would've stayed in a heartbeat.

Jackie asked her to go, though, and Ellie knew from her own experiences that processing traumatic events sometimes required solitary introspection. At least while a person licked their wounds.

Still, abandoning Jackie in her home after delivering more terrible news didn't sit well with her. She lifted her gaze to the rearview mirror. The LaPierre mansion glared back, gloomy beneath the dusky sky.

Ellie flipped the mirror up to escape the sadness as she pressed on the gas pedal. The road to the main gate of the LaPierre property, so peaceful and bright the last time she visited, seemed strange and shadowed.

Even the willow trees looked menacing, with their limbs swaying in the wind like skeletal hands reaching for the SUV.

21

Fading streaks of orange and purple painted the sky as dusk descended upon Charleston. Dying rays of sunlight crept between the city's buildings while Ellie drove to her parents' house. The dim headlights cast harsh and ominous shadows across the streets, ones that expanded and merged before her eyes.

Tilting forward in the driver's seat, she gazed at the clouds and colors as they mixed and mingled in the dimming light. By the time she rolled around the circular driveway in front of her family's mansion and shifted the vehicle into park, the sky had completed its metamorphosis into an inky-blue blanket of night.

"Thanks for picking me up and giving me a ride home." In the passenger seat, Helen unclicked her seat belt.

"You needed a break. Besides, Dad's still there."

Ellie read between the lines of her own words...*just in case*.

She swallowed hard. "What about Blake? I haven't seen him yet."

Helen rubbed her temple. "He was out running some errands for me, but said he'd sit with your father during the night."

That was a relief, at least.

There'd been no change in Dan's condition, good or bad. He remained motionless on his hospital bed, stuck in a medically induced coma until the doctors could figure out what was attacking his body.

How can they not figure out what's wrong with him?

Anxiety, with its tiny talons of unease sharpened to ultrafine points, gnawed at her nerves, shredding the fibers more and more each minute her brother lingered in his coma.

As they approached the front steps, Ellie's gaze fell on her mother. Deep shadows pooled in the hollows of Helen's face, giving her visage a ghastly skeletal shape. Exhaustion and worry were taking a heavy toll on her mother. Too heavy.

The doctors have to fix Dan. I don't know if my family will survive if he dies. Mom or Dad.

Greta greeted them at the door. Her frizzy silver-and-brown hair was down for once, held back by a floral headband. The colors matched the soft lines in the fabric of the jacket and skirt she wore over her white blouse. A red scarf circling her slim neck, combined with the new hairstyle, gave her a youthful vibe. In all the years Ellie had known Greta, this was the most relaxed she'd ever appeared.

At least one person in the house wasn't falling apart.

As Ellie and her mother stepped into the foyer, Greta shut the front door behind them. "Mrs. Kline, I'm so sorry. How's Dan?"

"He's still here, still fighting." Helen offered a weak smile, which was swiftly replaced by a steely expression of confidence. In a second, her back straightened and her chin jutted high. Her demeanor spoke volumes. *Challenge accepted.* "Knowing Dan, he'll beat this and come out tougher."

Ellie choked back tears. Her mother was so vulnerable and strong at the same time. *How does she do it? I shove my pain down and slap on a brave face. That's how I keep my strength, but Mom's strength comes from her pain. It's like the hurt fuels her will to defeat it.*

"You must be famished." Greta's gaze flitted to Ellie. "Both of you. Louis has whipped up a selection of sandwiches in the kitchen."

Ellie's stomach growled. Louis, her mother's personal chef, worked magic with two pieces of bread and a handful of condiments. "She's right, Mom."

"I can't eat." Helen placed a hand over her abdomen. "I won't. Not now."

"Mom. You need to stay strong. For Dan. And you can't stay strong on an empty stomach. Let's try to eat at least a bite or two."

Ellie grasped her mother's hand and led her down the long hallway to the kitchen. She turned to Greta, who trailed behind them. "Thank you, Greta. For picking up Bethany today and keeping her safe."

Greta's mouth curved into a gracious smile, her round cheeks a stark contrast to her square chin. "Absolutely. She's a pleasure."

Ellie wrapped an arm around Helen's shoulders and squeezed. "And thank you. For suggesting Greta pick up Bethany." Her mother's solution to Ellie's childcare problem while at the hospital had removed a ton of stress.

Helen said nothing but leaned her head against Ellie's shoulder and patted her hand.

They turned a corner into the kitchen, where Louis hovered near the stove with his hands clasped in front of his charcoal apron. He bowed his head, the pure white of his hair clashing against the deep bronze of his skin. "Mrs. Kline, please let me know if you would prefer to eat something different. I will make whatever you wish."

"Thank you, Louis." Helen stopped to examine the tray of sandwiches he'd set out on the kitchen island. "This looks wonderful."

Ellie ushered her mom toward the wooden table in the breakfast nook. "Sit. I'll bring you over a plate and something to drink."

Louis produced two glasses of sweet tea, carrying them to the table while Ellie perused the variety of sandwiches. She selected a chicken salad on wheat for her mom and a ham and turkey on white for herself, setting both down on the plates Louis provided.

"It's nice to get away from the hospital. At least for a little bit." Helen picked up the chicken-salad sandwich and nibbled as she stared out the window into the night. The moon offered just enough light to make out the silhouettes of the ornamental marigolds and zinnias outside. "I can't stay long, though. I have to be there. For Danny."

"Yeah. Of course. I understand."

Ellie scooted into a seat next to her mother. She scarfed her food down and sipped on her sweet tea, gazing at the tray of remaining sandwiches on the counter. Her voracious appetite begged for another to stifle her worry. Food always comforted her in times of distress.

No. I can't believe I'm even considering being so insensitive. Dan's in the hospital, and Mom's this close to shattering into a billion pieces, and all I can think about is how amazing Louis's homemade brown mustard tastes on these sandwiches.

She squeezed her stomach tight, patting her midsection to silence a growl. She'd stop at a drive-through on the way home. Double cheeseburgers and large fries all around. *Promise.* "What was the last update on Dan? Anything new?"

"No, not yet." Helen surveyed Ellie, the wrinkles around her lips stretching outward like delicate spiderwebs. "If you're hungry, you can get another sandwich. I won't be offended."

Ellie's jaw fell open. *Busted.* Snapping her mouth shut, she dropped her hands into her lap like a toddler in trouble, although she wasn't exactly sure why.

The corners of her mother's lips twitched upward, the closest action to a genuine smile she'd made in days. "I'm your mother. You think I don't know you eat when you're stressed? At least, more than you usually inhale in a sitting. You thought I forgot about all the pizzas and ice cream before, during, and after your senior year finals?"

"And the brownies. Can't forget about those." Ellie dipped her head, attempting to hide the grin sneaking across her face. "The poor delivery guy from that bakery with the supersized frosted ones was driving over here three times a day until the grades came in."

Helen reached under the table and gripped Ellie's hand. "It's okay to worry, and, like you told me ten minutes ago, it's okay to eat. Dan will be fine. I know he will. The doctors are running every test they can think of."

"Have they gotten any results back?" Ellie lifted her head. "Did they find illicit substances in Dan's blood?"

"Illicit what?" She snatched her hand back and reached for her sandwich. "Your brother does not use drugs, Eleanor. How could you make such a suggestion?"

Oh no.

"Not drugs like *illegal* drugs. I know Dan's not that type of guy. All I'm saying is, Dan was at the mayor's fundraising party, and whoever killed Monique isn't afraid to…" Ellie clamped her mouth shut.

This isn't another detective I'm talking to. It's Mom.

"What?" Her mother dropped her barely eaten sandwich on the plate, her face paling. "You...you think the person who hurt Monique tried to harm Dan too?"

Double oh no. Too much information for Mom.

Ellie's ears burned as she struggled to find the best words to undo what she'd already said. "Honestly, we aren't positive of anything right now. We begin each case with a number of working theories."

"We? You're working Monique's case? Why didn't you mention that before?" Helen stood, raised her hand to her forehead, and shambled to the kitchen door. "I'm...going to my room. I need a moment alone."

Ellie closed her eyes and scrunched her face. This case was too personal. She knew better than to discuss details from work with her parents. The less they knew, the more tolerant they were about her chosen career path. In this case, though, the victims were hitting too close to home.

At least, for her mom.

Helen Kline lost a friend three days ago. Now her son was in a coma, and no one knew what was attacking his body. Of course she was a mess. Ellie had added to the pile by revealing the possibility that Monique's killer also targeted Dan.

Why didn't I keep my mouth shut?

She rubbed tiny circles into her temples. The damage was done. The tidbit of information she unveiled would keep bouncing around her mother's mind. Taunting her while she waited by her son's bedside for either the doctors to cure him or for Dan to...

Ellie's throat dried up. *No. Don't think about that.*

Exhausted, she rose from the table and returned the sandwich plate to Louis. "Could you pack up a few of those to take to Dad? I doubt he's eaten anything in a while."

He accepted the dish with a silent nod. "Of course, Miss Kline."

"I'm going to run upstairs and get Beth packed up to go home. If Mom comes back down, can you keep her company until I get back?" She headed for the hall.

"Yes. I'll keep an ear and eye out for Mrs. Kline and distract her if needed until you return with little Miss Bethany."

Stopping in the kitchen doorway, she glanced back at the chef. His lips pursed and his brows knitted together in worry. "And Louis? Thank you for your help with Beth. And with Mom."

Crinkles formed beneath his sad eyes. "You're welcome."

On her way up the curving staircase, Ellie's phone buzzed in her pocket. She leaned her back against the railing and held the device up to her ear, stopping midway to the top landing. "Hi, Clay."

"Hey." An undercurrent of concern belied his casual greeting. "How's Dan?"

Ellie dug her fingernails into her palm. The pain from the burgeoning half-moon impressions distracted her from the fear building in her chest whenever she remembered Dan could die. "Nothing's changed. They still don't know what's making him sick."

"Is he still in a coma?"

"Yes." She bumped her toe against the bottom of the rail bordering the stairwell, and the mahogany stairs creaked beneath her shoe. She pressed her nails harder against her palm, breaking skin. Clay's worry for Dan touched her, but she needed to talk about something besides her brother. "We've discovered some interesting information regarding the case. Monique was pregnant."

"What?" Clay sounded as shocked as she'd felt. "You're kidding."

"Nope. We're trying to get cheek swabs from the men at the party. It's likely the father was in attendance."

Clay clicked his tongue. "This case keeps getting weirder and weirder. I've been crawling down the Delecroix Logistics rabbit hole all afternoon. My buddy at the treasury is working his magic on a few phantom accounts and shell corporations, but so far, we aren't having much luck."

"Which is exactly what we seem to need to solve this case. Luck." Upstairs, a tiny sneeze erupted. Bethany. Ellie's chest tightened. *How much does she know about what's going on?* "I gotta go. Talk to you later, okay?"

Before continuing on to Bethany's room, Ellie paused outside her mother's bedroom. Rustling noises came from inside. Drawers opened and closed. Knowing her mom, Helen Kline was packing a change of clothes and other necessities for Ellie's dad and herself.

She's preparing for the long haul. Ellie's heart sank. *Or the worst.* Resting her head on the wall, she fought back tears.

"Ellie?" Bethany's voice nearly made her jump out of her skin.

She twirled and found the little girl peeking out from behind her bedroom door. Wiping her eyes with the heel of her hand, Ellie plastered on the best happy expression she could muster. "How are you feeling, kiddo? You look down."

Bethany's blond braids dangled over the sleeves of her denim overall shorts and polka dotted t-shirt. She chewed her bottom lip, a small furrow forming between her brows. "Does your case have anything to do with Uncle Dan?" Her voice was tinged with a vulnerability too heavy for her eight years.

Dang it. This kid is so smart.

Ellie crouched and brushed a loose strand of hair around Bethany's ear, feeling the weight of her words before she spoke. "Maybe. We're not sure yet."

The child's dark-brown eyes, usually so full of mischief and wonder, widened with concern. "What if the bad guy comes after you? Or me and Nana?" Her small hand twisted the hem of her shirt, betraying her anxiety.

Ellie dropped to the floor, crisscrossing her legs and wrapping her arms around Bethany as she folded the little girl into her lap. The scent of Bethany's strawberry shampoo was a sweet reminder of innocence in a conversation far too grown-up.

"I'm not going to lie to you. I don't know what'll happen. Sometimes, bad people might come after us. What you have to remember is that we…Nana, me, and you…we've battled darkness before and kicked its butt. We're strong women, and whatever challenges we meet, we face them head-on."

Bethany sank into Ellie's chest. "I don't feel very strong." She punched a limp fist into the air. A braided band of purple, green, and blue string in a candy cane pattern encircled her wrist. The bracelet seemed to embody her spirit—vibrant yet fragile.

Ellie kissed the top of her head, an idea sparking. "How about we help you find that strength? We could sign you up for karate or tae kwon do this summer. Would that make you feel stronger?"

The transformation was immediate. Bethany's face brightened, her eyes regaining a glint of their usual spark. "Yes! I'd love that."

Ellie tapped Bethany's wrist. "Where'd you get this?"

Bethany held her arm out to admire the colorful bracelet. "Lyndy gave it to me. It's a friendship bracelet."

"Yeah?" Ellie rested her head on top of Bethany's. "I used to make those. I could show you how to make one to give to Lyndy. If you want."

"Really? That'd be awesome." Bethany burrowed her head

into Ellie's shoulder and hugged her tight. "And paper and pen, remember?"

"I remember."

The pair sat on the floor of the hallway for a long time, snuggling each other, until Ellie gathered enough courage to face the real world again.

22

After Kirra Long shoved her laptop into a desk drawer, using a tiny key to lock a latch beside the handle, she stood and straightened her jacket. A clank reverberated through LaPierre Foundation's halls and between the cracks of her closed office door. She paused, straining to catch another sound.

Stark silence was her only response.

She shrugged and patted her hair. It was probably the cleaning crew dropping a mop or something.

Slinging her designer bag over her shoulder, Kira checked the time on her diamond-studded watch. It was already after ten. Since Monique's death, she'd clocked out late every night, but not because she was doing any extra work. Even before Monique's untimely demise, Kira was the one holding the LaPierre Foundation and its activities together.

Her problem was the little fires that continued to pop up again and again. The ones that refused to fade away. Now that the police were sticking their noses into the foundation's business, she was about to lose her mind.

Speaking of which, that's one fire I need to put out. Immediately.

She retrieved her phone from her shoulder bag and dialed a number. The call rang six times before someone picked up. She kept her voice sharp and firm. "We have a problem. The police were here today, asking a lot of questions."

"What did you tell them?"

She flipped the light switch and locked her office door behind her. "Are you kidding? I'm not some newbie. I didn't tell them a thing." The tapping of her heels echoed off the walls as she walked through the empty lobby and out the building doors.

Outside, the warm and sticky night greeted her. The barest of breezes wisped around her and vanished back into the darkness. She strode along the sidewalk leading to the parking garage behind the building while sweat leaked from her pores. With her free hand, she fanned her face.

"What did they ask?"

She ignored the question. "I'm telling you, it's under control. At least for now. Thanks to me. I didn't share any information with them about our clients, but they threatened to get a warrant." Her phone jiggled against her cheek with each step she took.

A muffled expletive burst from the receiver.

Kira grimaced, holding the device away from her ear.

Rude.

She didn't appreciate being cursed at like this problem was hers and hers alone. If this was how it was going to be when the chips were down, she was done being the point of contact on this.

No more Ms. Nice Girl.

"Look, if they come back with a warrant, they'll have carte blanche access to the files. That's a problem for you, me, and everyone else. You get that, right? If you want to prevent that from happening, *you* need to do whatever it takes to get that warrant request squashed. Capisce?"

"Me? What exactly do you think I can do? I'm…"

Kira dragged her hand across her sweaty face as the tirade continued. She was over the complaints. The failures.

You'd think I'm the only one with a stake in this.

Bending down, she wiped her wet palm against her pants. "Shut up and listen to me." She lowered her voice to a hushed whisper. "We're both in danger here, and I'm not the one in a unique position to handle this issue. You are. You *will* take care of the warrant *now*. Monique's murder is shining too bright a light on us. *All* of us."

And we're scrambling like roaches to hide.

Kira kept the roaches bit to herself and hung up, refusing to listen to one more complaint. She slipped the phone back into her bag and continued toward the parking garage. Maybe it was time to cut her losses and take off? She'd saved up a good chunk of change. Enough to get out of the country and start over.

A faraway cough stopped Kira short, and she gazed into the darkness. Shallow breaths rolled in and out of her mouth, and she forced her lips together so she could hear better. She tugged at the collar of her blouse, wishing another baby breeze would brush past her. Her hand fanned her face with more frantic motions.

She was close to a nervous breakdown.

Ever since Monique died, the tension around LaPierre was like the cough syrup they passed out to needy families in winter. Thick and sticky enough to coat a spoon. Toss in the dreadful humidity, and it was no wonder she was so wound up. Sweat pooled between her brows as she strained her ears, trying to catch another sound.

Silence enveloped her. The trees stood still, like soldiers

waiting for inspection. Even the damned crickets stopped chirping.

She kicked into action, walking faster down the sidewalk. The second she reached the narrow stairwell to the upper levels at the side of the parking garage, Kira hurried upward. The rapid *tap-tap* of her heels rose higher and higher, until she was halfway up.

A *clomp*, heavy and abrupt, rose from a section of the garage beneath her.

What was that?

The shadows clawed at her. As she cast a nervous glance behind her, Kira's heart beat so fast and hard she was certain the organ would shoot right out of her chest. She peered down the stairwell, holding her breath. The bottom landing remained empty.

I know I heard a footstep. I know it.

She proceeded up the stairs backward and stopped again. The click of a door shutting floated up the corridor. Tingles shot up and down Kira's rigid spine, her wide eyes glued to the bottom landing.

Someone's down there. Maybe someone leaving?

She steadied herself and waited for the roar of a car engine and the squeal of tires against concrete. Paranoia overwhelmed her more and more each passing second. Blood pounded in her ears, dulling her hearing.

Or someone coming. For me.

Kira spun and raced up the stairs, her heels slamming against each step. At the top, she shoved her shoulder into the door and barreled into the third level of the garage. She half sprinted, half walked to her car, every sense on red alert.

A muffled *clank* snuck up behind her. She whirled, staring at the exit door to the stairwell.

What the hell was that noise?

The door remained closed, taunting her with stubborn

silence. Beneath her tight suit jacket, her chest heaved. She unbuttoned the fabric and inhaled as the sides flew open. The silk shirt underneath was soaked in sweat.

Voices carry.

Kira laughed, surprised her mind was rationalizing the noises with an old eighties song. The song was accurate, though. Sounds carried themselves across great distances. Any of the things she'd heard could have originated from anywhere in the expansive garage.

She was safe. Just paranoid as hell.

Turning away from the door, she walked toward her car, pressing the button on the key fob to unlock her luxury BMW. Relieved, she released the breath stuck in her lungs.

And sucked that breath back in.

In her periphery, she spotted movement. The hair on the back of her neck stood, and she squeezed her eyes shut. *Just your imagination.* She twirled and opened her eyes, shocked to find an actual person stepping out from the shadows.

A strangled gasp jumped out of Kira's throat. As she stumbled backward, one of her heels wiggled against the concrete, threatening to twist her ankle. Flinging her arms out, she regained her footing.

The person shrouded in the darkness moved, slow and steady.

Kira hobbled closer. "Leave me alone." The person's size and shape were familiar, but she couldn't quite place why.

Without a word, he stepped forward. Though the garage was dim, the scant light still reflected off the glinting knife in the man's fist.

Oh, fuck no.

Kira's heart crashed into her throat. She twisted around and ran, fumbling with the key fob of her BMW and pressing the button over and over. The *beep-beep-beep* of the car's security system blasted in front of her.

All I have to do is get to my car. God, please let me make it.

Behind her, shoes squeaked each time the soles smacked the floor. She refused to look back.

Once the squeaks caught up to her, a large, strong hand grabbed her arm, forcing her to flounder to a stop. She opened her mouth to scream.

If I'm lucky, maybe someone else is in the parking garage. Someone who can help.

As soon as she finished her thought, a hand clamped over her mouth. Kira reached backward, scratching and pawing at the air. Her fingers latched on to the fabric of a black hoodie. She lunged forward and tugged hard, trying to disengage the man from her body.

Without warning, a sharp pain sliced through her back. She choked on a scream, and her knees went weak. Another cut separated the flesh in her side. She grasped at the area, her hand trembling as she looked down. In a daze, she studied the red substance spreading across her silk blouse like watercolor on a wet canvas.

She began to shake violently, her legs giving out and bringing her assailant to the ground with her.

Bile surged up her throat as she fought to keep her body's liquids in place. Her hand pressed against her belly, but the blood refused to stop. She struggled to gulp the vomit back down, hurling when the man continued his assault.

Kira gagged and gurgled in agony as the knife plunged into her torso.

Over and over and over.

23

Butter bubbled in the skillet as Ellie cracked three eggs on the edge of a mixing bowl, one by one. She tossed in a pinch of pepper, pausing for a second to inhale the fresh, fiery aroma.

When she was younger, Ellie and a girl from her class had attempted to bake cookies in Ellie's enormous kitchen. They were too short to reach all the ingredients, but they'd solved that issue by pushing a chair into the walk-in pantry and rummaging around. After grabbing the items they thought they needed, they plopped them into a bowl and mixed until their elbows ached.

Their mothers found them before they turned the oven on. After dumping the whole mix down the garbage disposal, their mothers pulled out stools for them to stand on and taught Ellie and her friend the proper way to bake cookies.

One ingredient she and the other girl chose for their sugar bowl monstrosity was pepper. The reason was unclear now, but ever since then, the scent always took her back to that day.

Bethany leaned over the counter to supervise, balancing on a wobbly stool. "Now what?"

"We whisk. Do you want to do the honors?" Ellie retrieved a metal whisk from a drawer and held the utensil up.

"Oh, yeah." Bethany rubbed her hands together like she was about to enter a fierce competition before accepting the utensil. She set the balloon end into the bowl, and a soft splash erupted from the mixture. Her hand flew in wild circles, whisking with abandon like an unhinged turbine.

"Whoa…easy there, killer." Ellie positioned herself behind the little girl and placed her hand over Bethany's. Together, they moved the whisk in gentle but speedy circles.

Ellie giggled to herself. *Like Demi and Patrick, but without the romance. Or pottery.*

"You have to be more mindful of the stir. Otherwise, you'll beat the eggs to death and wear them to school."

"Okay, I get it." Bethany slowed down. Ellie relaxed and removed her hand.

When Ellie's phone vibrated in her pocket, she gave Bethany a thumbs-up. "That's perfect. Keep doing exactly that for a second. I've got a call."

"Good morning." Jillian appeared in the doorway, her arms raised above her head in a deep stretch. Her blond hair fell over the shoulders of her sleep shirt as her arms relaxed. Once she stepped into the kitchen, her eyes lit up. "Ooh, eggs."

"We've got one in there for you." Ellie squeezed her roommate's arm gently and lowered her voice. "Watch Beth for a sec, okay?"

Jillian saluted her. "Roger that."

Ellie moved into the hall and lifted the phone to her ear. "Detective Kline."

Lancaster's gruff voice cut through the laughter in the

kitchen behind her. "They've found another body. Wanna guess whose?"

She sighed and pinched the bridge of her nose. *There go my morning plans with Bethany.* "Just tell me."

"Kira Long."

"What?" They'd only spoken to her the day before. *How can she be dead? And why?*

"Yep. And of all the murders, this one's the most violent." Lancaster clicked his tongue. "Way more vicious than Monique's or Bernard's death."

With another sigh, Ellie kicked off her fuzzy slippers. "I'm on my way."

After jotting down the crime scene address and ending the call, she trudged back into the kitchen.

Bethany held the bowl over the skillet while Jillian used a spatula to scrape the egg mixture out. When Ellie returned, Jillian frowned. "Uh-oh. Duty calls?"

Ellie locked eyes with Bethany. The little girl pouted and gave Ellie her best Puss in Boots imitation.

Dammit all.

"I'm afraid so." Ellie ran her fingers through her wild locks.

Bethany lowered her gaze before setting the bowl on the counter. "It's okay. I can go to school with Nana and Papa or something."

This sucks so much.

Ellie walked over and slid her arm around Bethany. Asking her parents to drop Bethany at school was off the table. They needed to focus on Dan. "How about I call Clay instead?"

Jillian waved her hands in the air. "What am I? Chopped liver?" She wrapped an arm around Bethany's shoulders. "How about you and I finish this epic breakfast? Then we can listen to your favorite tunes and belt them out at the top of our lungs on the way to school. I'll even let you listen to the grown-up songs. What do you say?"

Bethany clapped her hands in delight. "Really?"

Ellie chewed on her lip, waffling. "Didn't you and Jake have plans this morning? I can't ask you to cancel on him."

Jillian shook her head. "That's not even an issue. Do what you need to do. Bethany and I—"

"And Schneider." Bethany pointed at her stuffed walrus perched on the counter by a box of crackers. In the weeks since Clay gifted her the toy, she'd grown very attached. "Don't forget about him."

Jillian grinned. "And Schneider. We have everything under control here. You go do what you do best."

Ellie grasped her best friend's hands. "I owe you one."

"I know." Jillian's smile dwindled when she eyed the skillet. Gasping, she shoved the rubber spatula into the solidifying egg mixture.

Ellie peeked over her friend's shoulder. The eggs were already crisp on the bottom.

Jillian tapped a finger against her bottom lip. "Bethany, I think we have one or two slices of cheese in the refrigerator. Be a doll and grab them for me. We're having omelets instead of scrambled eggs."

Bethany hopped off her stool and skipped to the refrigerator. There were exactly two cheese slices left on the shelf. She carried the package over to the counter.

"See? Everything's under control." Jillian wiped her hands on her nightshirt and shooed Ellie away. "Now go. We've got a busy morning ahead of us. And so do you."

❄

Half an hour later, Ellie strode toward the crime scene. The spot hummed with the activity of buzzing forensic investigators identifying evidence with yellow markers. Uniformed officers stood guard at the edge of the chaos.

Once she caught sight of Lancaster, she ducked under the crime scene tape. After she signed the logbook, one of the techs handed her a pair of gloves and booties. She slipped them on and scanned the scene.

A black, circular dome in the parking garage ceiling caught her eye. When she approached Lancaster, Ellie gestured to the dome. "We need to lock down any security footage immediately."

He tore his gaze from the victim to glance at her. "Already on it. Security has the tape ready for us, whenever you want to head down and take a peek."

Ellie paused above Kira Long's body. The corpse's wide open and bloodshot eyes stared into nothingness. Burst capillaries dotted her face like dozens of red ants. The elegant brocade suit she'd worn the day before crinkled over her stiff body, the crevices of the pattern stained with crimson splatters.

Jagged rips in her silk blouse were stressed with larger stains and trails of vomit. Strands of Kira's long hair sprawled out, stiff and matted in a large pool of coagulating blood around her back and head.

Just yesterday, she was the picture of perfection, with her pressed suit and well-coiffed hairstyle. Now she's lying in a puddle of her own blood on the floor of a parking garage. What happened?

Lancaster bent over Kira. "Medical examiner says she was stabbed repeatedly. About six or seven times. The perp left bloodied footprints on his way back to the stairwell."

"Trackable?" Ellie crouched and stared into Kira's dead eyes.

"Partially. About halfway down the stairwell, they fade away too much to track. I've got forensics analyzing the boot prints to determine the model and type." Lancaster stood and rubbed his nose with his inner arm. "They're estimating TOD to be sometime late last night, but the M.E. will need to confirm the exact time once she has her on the table."

Ellie rose while she considered the relationship between the recent crimes. "This has to be connected to Monique LaPierre. Two people linked to the LaPierre Foundation dying within days of each other isn't a coincidence. Three, if you include the security guard from the Coastline Inn."

"You and I are on the same page."

"What about Quint Bannister?" Ellie surveyed the yellow markers and blood splatters dotting the concrete.

"Haven't heard anything back on him yet." Lancaster's attention shifted toward the purr of an airplane flying overhead, somewhere above the parking garage. "I suspect, though, that he might've received assistance from LaPierre in his youth. He fits the profile of struggling during his upbringing and still making it into functional society."

"Okay. Let's go down to the security office and see about that footage." As they walked to the edge of the crime scene and dipped under the tape, Ellie snapped off her gloves. "After, you should make tracking down Bannister's history priority number one. I need to investigate Donna Montague some more. Those two are involved somehow. I can feel it."

Jackie too.

Although her friend possessed no motive to kill Kira—that Ellie knew of—she still couldn't officially eliminate the woman from the suspects list. After all, Jackie was receiving an impressive inheritance from her mother's death. Ellie would be more relieved once she irrevocably cleared Jackie. Plus, the way their discussion had ended the night before pecked at her heart like a vulture over a fresh kill.

She rolled her shoulders, trying to shrug the guilt away. "How are the cheek swabs going?"

"I've made a few calls and set up some appointments.

We've got someone at the precinct ready to work with people as they come in to get the swab taken, labeled, and categorized." Lancaster's tone softened and he halted his stride. "I've got this handled, you know. You can relax."

"Relax?" A hot flush swept over Ellie's cheeks, followed by a violent churn in her belly.

Relax?

She pictured her mother, frail and afraid, hovering over Dan's bedside.

Relax? Really?

Ellie stepped closer to Lancaster, her model's height matching his own six-foot frame almost eye to eye. "This guy may've tried to hurt my brother. Simply handling these tasks will not catch this guy. He's crafty and dangerous. I can't relax, and you need to get this more than handled."

Frustration darkened his features. Without another word, he brushed past her and stomped off in the direction of the security office.

Ellie stayed put and tried to rein in her temper. The heat in her cheeks changed from anger to embarrassment. Her words were harsh, she knew that. There was too much at stake for her family for him to drag his feet on this case, though.

Dan was in trouble, and her options to save him were disappearing.

The bastard who murdered Monique, Bernard, and Kira had gone after her brother once already. Who was to say he wouldn't target him again? If the doctors couldn't figure out what was wrong with him, she had to find the killer and make him tell her what he used to drug her brother. He was the key to saving Dan.

Her stomach sloshed. *I have to catch this guy. Fast.*

Time was running out for her family.

24

Black-and-white television screens covered the wall of the security section in the parking garage's central control room, which was so small that fitting five or six people inside was impossible. Ellie shoved a wooden wedge under the door, locking it at a ninety-degree angle toward the outer concrete wall of the first level.

A water cooler near the door burped air bubbles as the security guard pushed the lever down and filled up a paper cup.

He gulped the drink and crushed the cup, tossing the container into a bin under his desk. "What's the time frame you need?" He then popped a stick of minty gum into his mouth, slid into his chair, and flipped on a tiny desk fan.

Hunching forward, Ellie placed a hand on the back of his chair. "Late last night. Say, around ten?" She glanced at Lancaster.

He nodded but didn't meet her gaze.

Her cheeks grew hot as she recalled her outburst minutes earlier. In the moment, the passion seemed necessary. In hindsight, Ellie knew she'd overreacted. She owed Lancaster an apology, but mending fences in work situations? Not her greatest skill.

She returned her focus to the screens.

The guard brought the cameras online and clicked buttons, scrolling through the footage. "Just let me know when you want me to stop. This camera is positioned outside, at the bottom of the main stairwell."

Several minutes of video sped by before Kira Long popped up. Ellie pointed at the screen. "There. Stop and play there."

Lancaster crossed his arms and moved in closer, peering at the footage.

While Kira walked, she held a phone to her ear. The conversation appeared heated, not casual. Her facial expressions contorted from annoyance to anger in a matter of seconds, and her walking speed increased as the call continued. At one point, she held the phone at arm's length, like the person was too loud. Or screaming.

"Phone records." Ellie shifted toward Lancaster. "We need to find out who was on the other end of that call. Especially since it was so close to her time of death."

While Lancaster retrieved a notebook from his pocket and scribbled down her directive, he still refused to make eye contact.

She crossed her arms. *Well, he's going to be a tough nut to crack back open.*

The guard continued playing the video. When Kira entered the stairwell, he switched the screen to a different camera angle. Kira hustled up the steps, pausing halfway and craning her neck like she was waiting. A few more seconds passed, and she continued up the stairs and out of the shot.

After a couple clicks of the mouse, the footage switched to a third camera. The guard bobbed his head. "We're inside the garage now."

Ellie readjusted to stare closer at the screen. "Is this the only angle we have?" Concrete columns blocked the view as Kira swept through to the far side of the garage. Above her, glowing orbs provided a dull light over the mostly empty parking spaces.

"Theoretically, we have three cameras covering this area inside of the garage. Besides the one we're currently looking at, there's another camera over here in the garage layout." He gestured to an area in the corner of the screen they were watching. "But it's out of commission right now."

"Why?" As Ellie squinted at the area he indicated, she made out a dome shape similar to the one she detected earlier at the crime scene. "Don't you guys need these in working order for insurance or something?"

He shrugged, chomping his gum. "The thing just died one day, and they haven't replaced it yet."

"Okay..." Ellie drummed her fingers against the back of his chair and released a drawn-out sigh. "What about the third one?"

The guard dragged his finger to another screen, above the one they'd been viewing, where the calf of Kira's leg was visible. "This other camera isn't going to help much unless she moves more to the left. So yeah, the screen we're looking at is the only angle we've got."

Ellie stifled a groan and clenched her jaw. *Of all the rotten luck. Three cameras, and only one's useful.* "Then keep going with what we've got."

Kira vanished around a column and reappeared near a BMW. The headlights and taillights blinked on the vehicle, but she didn't get in. She remained outside, staring into an ill-lit spot near the garage wall. Her feet scurried forward until she was seven or eight feet away from the hood of her car.

"Pause the footage. Right there." Ellie leaned over the

security guard's shoulder and tapped the middle of the screen. "There. Do you see it?"

The guard smacked his gum and slouched closer. His head tilted. "I'll be damned. Is that a person?"

Footage showed a head poking out from behind a column. The figure hid in the shadows where Kira's attention was focused, wearing a dark hoodie, obscuring their face.

Ellie stared at the black-and-white pixels until her vision blurred. *Dammit. I can't make anything out of this mess except for a big blob.*

Lancaster grunted and scribbled in his notebook. "Why is the garage so dim there? And why is the footage grainy?"

The scent of spearmint filled the room when the guard spoke. "Beats me, man. I don't buy the cameras. Some of the lights were smashed out a week ago. Management hasn't gotten around to replacing them. I had to go clean up the broken glass. Freaking good thing whoever was responsible picked a spot no one had parked in."

Ellie glanced at Lancaster. "One of the cameras is down, and our perp is hiding in an area where the lights were knocked out. Coincidence?"

He shook his head. "I don't know. Another scenario is that our guy was here, noticed the camera down and the lights out, and saw an opportunity."

There's one way to find out.

She returned her attention to the guard. "Did you get any footage of the lights being smashed out?"

"Yeah, actually. A group of kids. Probably some delinquents from LaPierre. We couldn't ID any of them. No one at the foundation would help us out."

Ellie blew a thin strand of hair out of her face. "Okay. Continue playing."

On the screen, Kira paused and spoke to the figure. Why wouldn't she turn and run right away?

"Is there sound?" Ellie rested her palms on the desk as she focused on the mass of black-and-white pixels. Did Kira know who the person was and not feel threatened?

The guard sighed and paused the footage. "Sorry, no sound."

Damn. "All right. Keep going."

The figure lurched forward. Kira stumbled, regained her footing, and ran. Lights flashed from the BMW in a flurry of waves and bounced off an object in the figure's hand.

A knife.

The killer caught up with Kira and pounced. Ellie sucked in a hard breath as she watched Kira squirm and fight back. Before the woman even knew what hit her, the murderer rammed the blade into her back.

After another stab, Kira violently convulsed. The action knocked them both to the ground behind the car. For several moments, the footage showed no movement. Until the figure rose again, tugging at the hood twisted over his face. He slunk back into the shadows and retreated toward the stairwell.

Ellie straightened, her tone resolute. "He knew where the cameras were."

Lancaster slid his hands in his pockets and rocked back and forth on his heels. "My guess? He's visited this parking garage a lot. Enough to know the layout and see the opportunity."

"Can we run through the camera in the stairwell again? Earlier, though."

It's a long shot, but maybe we'll luck out. The guy had to get on the third level some way.

The guard's hand hovered over his mouse. "How early?"

"Start at six and fast-forward. We're looking for the guy in the hoodie."

The man clicked a few buttons and the stairwell camera popped onto the screen. Between six and seven thirty, several men and women in dressy suits and skirts traipsed up the stairs to the upper levels. The closer the time stamp got to ten p.m., the more Ellie's heart raced.

What are the other ways into the garage? If he didn't use the stairs, maybe there's an elevator?

At nine forty-five, the guard hit pay dirt. A person jogged up the stairs in a hoodie, head dipped low to ensure the cameras didn't catch a face. The guard fast-forwarded to after the murder. On the way down, the person's face was still concealed.

Drat.

Ellie pivoted toward Lancaster. "I estimate the perp is in their late twenties or early thirties. Caucasian, although the black-and-white screen makes it hard to tell. And maybe one hundred and ninety or two hundred pounds. That sound about right to you?"

He nodded. "Yeah."

"Good. We need to visit Kira's next of kin. Do we have information on that yet?"

Lancaster flipped through his notebook and reviewed a page. "Her parents are still alive, and they live nearby. From what I've gathered so far, Kira appears to have still lived with them. We could drive out there right now. She's also got a brother, but he's out West."

"What are we waiting for?" Ellie thanked the security guard for his help. "We'll need a copy of that footage, so I'll send an officer by for it."

If they were lucky, the tech department could clean it up enough to see the monster's face as they hid in the shadows.

After getting the address from Lancaster, she walked back

to her SUV. The driver's seat wheezed when she slid onto the hot leather. Ellie rolled the windows down and cranked the AC up to full blast.

Butterflies swirled in her stomach. She was often the bearer of bad news in her line of work, but the job never got easier.

No matter how many times she had to do it.

25

The Long home was situated in a neighborhood filled with winding roads and cookie-cutter ranch homes. Grassy, overgrown yards begging to be mowed bordered one or two. Ellie watched Lancaster maneuver around the cul-de-sac and pull to a stop in front of a royal blue house with white shutters and a minivan in the driveway.

She parked her SUV behind his Subaru and scrutinized the slice of middle-class heaven. Not the upper-class mini-mansion she'd expected from Kira's pricey accessories. Grabbing her belongings, she slipped out of the vehicle.

Lancaster crossed his arms as she approached. "I hate this part."

"Me too." Ellie walked ahead of him, down a stone walkway and up two steps onto the porch. The back of her neck tensed. Telling unsuspecting people a loved one was gone, someone they planned to call later or have over for dinner next Sunday, was never easy.

"So who's gonna be the bad guy here?" Lancaster joined Ellie on the porch.

"Could you?" Her heart raced as she eyed the door, hoping no one was home.

You've done this before...what's wrong with you?

He grunted his agreement. "Glad to know you trust me with something."

Ignoring the quip, she wrapped her fingers around a brass door knocker and rapped three times.

It's late morning. Someone should be up.

A *click* sounded on the other side, and the door eased open halfway. An older woman with bright-blue eyes peeked out. "Yes?"

Every muscle in Ellie's body tensed. *Just get the visit over with.* "Good morning. We'd like to speak with Melody Long, Kira Long's mother. Is that you?" She held up her badge.

The woman inched the door open a bit more. Her hawkish nose poked farther out. "Yes, I'm Kira's mom. Why? Has she done something wrong?"

We don't know yet. The only thing we're sure of is that she's gone. So very gone.

Ellie choked down a glob of saliva and pushed the words out of her mouth. "Mrs. Long, may we come inside and speak with you in private?"

The woman nodded and stepped aside, revealing a cozy living room with afghans tossed over the back of a tweed couch and family photos covering the walls. She shut the door behind them and motioned to the furniture. "Sit anywhere you'd like. I apologize for the mess."

Ellie scrutinized the controlled chaos in the room. Her own living room was well-organized with lots of open space and few extras beyond the couch and coffee table, whereas the Long living room rebelled against the mere suggestion of a minimalist lifestyle.

Random stacks of books protruded from every nook and cranny. Baskets of magazines sat next to the couch. Framed family photos hung alongside shelves filled with knickknacks and folk art. An oversize cat tree claimed two-thirds of the space in front of the picture window.

Despite the busy decor, jealousy tugged at Ellie's heart. This room was comfortable, and lived in, and loved. No room in her apartment gave off such a relaxed and happy feel. Except Bethany's. She eased onto a tweed couch cushion.

Lancaster chose a battered green armchair beside the couch. Melody settled into a wooden rocking chair across from him. She clamped her hands in her lap, her gaze shifting uneasily between the two detectives.

Ellie averted her eyes, unwilling to register the moment the news of Kira's death sank into the mother's chest.

Lancaster cleared his throat. "Mrs. Long, I'm very sorry. Your daughter is dead."

The woman scoffed. "No. No, she isn't. I talked to her yesterday. Or was it the night before? Anyway, she's fine. She's always fine."

He inhaled deeply, as if considering his next words carefully. "No, ma'am. I'm afraid we discovered Kira's body this morning. She's gone."

Ellie held her breath in the silence following Lancaster's statement, releasing it only after a strangled cry filled the room. Mrs. Long doubled over, the movement rocking her chair in staggered lurches.

Along with Lancaster, Ellie waited for the initial shock to subside.

"How did she die? No. Don't tell me." The older woman raised her head and scowled. "It was that place she worked at. She was such a nice girl, but she became a different person when she went to the LaPierre Foundation."

Ellie's ears perked up. "Different? How so?"

"She got uppity. Traded in her Toyota for a BMW. Started

wearing fancy clothes. You know, like Gucci and Balenci what's-his-name?" Mrs. Long tapped her fingertips on her temple. "Confused the heck out of her dad and me. She started acting like she was actually part of the rich elite. But she wasn't. She just worked for them. Kira even moved out of here and rented this ritzy apartment across town."

A ritzy apartment? The address on Kira's driver's license still showed the Long home as her place of residence. They needed to check that out as soon as possible. Her gaze met Lancaster's.

As if reading her mind, he nodded and asked for the address, jotting it in his notebook.

A cuckoo clock ticking in another room sprang to life, sending shrill chirps through the house. Eleven *cuckoos* later, the wooden bird retired back into its home. After the *pop* of a tiny door shutting, only the ticking remained.

Ellie scooted to the edge of the couch, getting closer to Kira's mother. "Was the apartment for show? You know, to keep up with the Joneses? Or was your daughter actually making enough money to comfortably afford the place?"

"I think she was making great money, so I doubt she got the place to enhance her image. Lately, she had gotten very *I want it, I'll get it*. Like that song? Lord knows how she was making her money, though." Mrs. Long blew her nose, her frown deepening. "The thing is, the LaPierre Foundation is a nonprofit. Legally, they've gotta share the executives' salaries. I've seen the list. Kira was making good money, but not *BMW* money."

"Is it possible the charity wasn't her only source of income?" Lancaster shifted in his seat and pulled out his notebook. He scribbled a couple notes onto the paper.

"I've wondered if she had some side gig but never asked." The older woman's shoulders slumped, and her eyes glistened. "Maybe I should have."

"What about boyfriends?" Ellie pinched a tissue from a box on a side table by the couch and handed it to Mrs. Long. "Was there someone in the picture who may have wanted to hurt Kira?"

Mrs. Long shredded the tissue in half. "I'm not sure. I know I said before that we'd spoken the other day, and we had, but our calls had gotten very short. And forget visits. I hadn't seen her in months. Her job at LaPierre ate up every blessed moment she had in the day. To be honest, I hadn't really been a part of her life recently. She changed and didn't fit in with us anymore, I guess." She dabbed her eyes and sniffed.

Ellie pursed her lips. Save for the cuckoo clock's intrusion, the house had been quiet the entire visit. "Is Mr. Long here?"

Mrs. Long shook her head. "No, he's out of town. Golfing trip with his buddies. I'll have to call and tell him to come on home." Her voice quavered, and the floodgates opened.

"Is there someone I can call to be with you now?"

She reached for another tissue. "My sister, but I'll call her myself."

Ellie exchanged a knowing look with Lancaster. Rising from the couch, she fished a business card out of her bag. "Mrs. Long, we won't take up any more of your time. If you think of anything else, please don't hesitate to call." She handed her contact info over to the grieving woman. "And again, I'm terribly sorry about your daughter."

Mrs. Long nodded, too consumed by sobs to respond.

"Are you sure I can't call your sister for you? I hate to leave you by yourself."

With what appeared to take tremendous effort, Mrs. Long composed herself. "I'll be okay. I'd actually like a few moments to myself before…you know."

Yes, Ellie did.

She squeezed the woman's hand. "Yes, it's not fair how much has to be done after something terrible like this."

When Ellie and Lancaster stepped outside, the woman closed the front door behind them. Her muffled wail caught up to Ellie before she could escape to the safety of her SUV. She pictured her own mother and father going through a similar reenactment if the worst happened to Dan Jr.

What if he didn't survive?

She'd never lived in a world without her big brother. Her stomach lurched.

No. He'll survive. He has to.

Ellie called out to Lancaster as he gripped the handle of his car door. "Can you go back to the precinct and try to get access to Kira's bank records? I'd like to see where her money was coming from."

He gave a thumbs-up in acknowledgment. "One step ahead of you. I'll also get the warrant for her ritzy apartment."

"Thanks. Let me know as soon as we've got it."

She climbed into her vehicle and fastened her seat belt. Dan would get better. He had the best doctors in the state doing all they could for him. Like her mom said, now their family had to play a waiting game.

In the meantime, Ellie intended to catch the bastard who put Dan Jr. in the hospital.

26

Ellie parallel parked into a space beside Kira's apartment complex and checked her reflection in the rearview mirror. Sweaty wisps of copper hair stuck to her face and neck. Yanking the hair tie off her wrist, she corralled her wild curls into a tight ponytail.

Lancaster was back at the precinct, checking on the bank and phone records for Kira Long and monitoring the status of the cheek swabs. When the call came in that the search warrant they'd requested for Kira's apartment was ready, he'd been away from his desk. She left him a sticky note telling him to meet her, but she didn't wait around for him to return.

Was she rude to leave him behind? Maybe. But she'd made it clear to Stoddard and Lancaster that flying solo was how she worked. A sticky note was more than generous notification.

She walked around the side toward the main entrance, taking in the view of the Ashley River at the end of the street as she cornered the building. *Riverfront view. Fancy.*

Inside, track lighting surrounded a chandelier in the

center of the ceiling. Cream-colored walls were set off by a floor of white brick and parquet tiles. The lobby included not one but two sitting areas. One faced the window with a view of a geometrical art piece in the courtyard. The other sat near a small library and featured a long marble table with various games like chess and checkers available for play.

Ellie wandered to a couple of rectangular pillars at the end of the room, where a desk with a retro bell sat between the columns. She slapped the bell and waited. The middle-aged, bearded man who answered her call mistook her for a prospective tenant until she produced the warrant and drew his attention to the badge on her belt.

He led her to a bank of polished elevators in the center of the lobby and up to the tenth floor, where he unlocked Kira's apartment. After Ellie muttered a *thanks*, she shut Kira's front door behind her.

At first glance, the apartment yielded nothing remarkable. Oversize windows with views of a park formed one wall. Solid wood floors in a pale-brown shade covered most of the room, save for a colorful rectangular rug positioned under a sandy-colored leather couch and matching armchairs.

The kitchen was a simple setup consisting of a white, marble-topped island, white cabinets, and stainless steel appliances. More marble decorated the bathroom walls and counters. Flanking one side of a double sink was a large soaking tub. A door Ellie presumed led to a toilet cubby was on the other side.

Overall, the apartment didn't appear as impressive as she expected. Kira seemed to live the luxurious life, though.

And above her means. The rent on this place is probably more than a couple grand a month. Maybe another several grand on furniture.

Decor-wise, the space was sparse.

Which made sense. If Kira spent so much on rent and living room sets, there wouldn't be much left over for extras.

Ellie strolled over to the balcony window where the glorious view of the Ashley River was dulled by the wilted and dry potted plants sprawled over the balcony floor. *Maybe they were left by the previous tenant? Kira didn't seem like the green thumb type when we met with her.*

Setting her bag on the kitchen island, Ellie pulled out a pair of latex gloves and stretched them over her hands.

Her first stop was a spiral-bound notebook splayed out on the kitchen counter. She eased the cover open. Haphazard numbers and letters spread across most of the paper. She turned the page. Similar numbers and letters, along with asterisks, covered the paper from edge to edge. On the sixth page, penciled-in columns of *X*s and *O*s ran beside the numbers and letters. While the rest of the pages were blank, Ellie noticed ripped strips of paper in the notebook's spiral, indicating the removal of some pages.

The letters were grouped in batches of twos and threes. *Initials, maybe?* The numbers spanned the four- to six-digit range. Asterisks spotted the paper, beside a letter here and a number there. None of the scribblings made sense, separate or as a whole. Whatever the letters and numbers meant, only Kira could decipher them.

A stack of mail and other scraps of paper on a side table by the couch caught Ellie's eye. She placed the notebook inside an evidence bag and crossed the room. Her tight gloves pinched her skin as she sifted through the receipts and envelopes. When she reached an opened bank statement, she stopped and slid the document out. Unfolding the paper, she studied the list of transactions.

Kira made some payments to a pricey law firm and received a direct deposit from LaPierre, which matched up with what Kira's mother told Ellie about Kira's salary. Good money, but not good enough to finance her lifestyle.

According to the charges on the statement, Kira enjoyed eating out and shopping at the most expensive boutiques in town. Often. At places where a dress and a pair of cute heels or a couple of bottles of wine and a steak would take at least half of her hefty paycheck from LaPierre.

Ellie ran her gloved fingertip down the statement and paused. Several payments for consulting fees leaped out at Ellie, each fee almost as much, or more, than Kira's actual paycheck. Melody Long was right...her daughter had a side gig.

As some kind of consultant.

Ellie dragged her finger to the payer information and nearly gasped.

Delecroix Logistics.

Blinking, she shook her head and examined the name again. It was the same company referenced in LaPierre Foundation's account history. The same company with shady business practices Clay claimed were protected by a ton of legal tape.

Delecroix Logistics was paying money to Kira Long.

Why? As a bribe, maybe?

As Ellie continued to inspect the apartment, a question haunted her.

What could Kira Long possibly have possessed that Delecroix valued so much?

27

As an icy chill swept through Charleston's city morgue, Ellie shuddered while she donned a pair of gloves and booties. Studying dead bodies wasn't how she envisioned spending her afternoon.

Doctor Faizal's call arrived right after Ellie finished her visit to Kira Long's apartment where, aside from the bank statements displaying huge payments made to Kira from Delecroix Logistics, she'd discovered zip. The moment the M.E.'s name popped up on her screen, any hope of joining Bethany for the afternoon vanished.

The M.E. stood in the autopsy room between two tables holding the bodies of Monique LaPierre and Bernard Cookson. She hunched over Bernard's corpse, studying his neck. Her white lab coat rustled against the metal table every time she moved.

A large smile spread across the other woman's face as Ellie approached. "Detective Kline. Long time, no see." She chuckled at her own joke. Tiny baby hairs sprouted beneath the braided crown of black tresses around her head.

Ellie rounded the table holding Bernard's body and

returned the grin. "I was glad to get your call. I didn't expect you to get back to me so quickly with information."

Doctor Faizal raised her hands and wiggled her slender fingers. "And I've got some interesting news, but first, the fetus. We've got blood tests and DNA screenings for both the fetus and Monique. Now we need candidates for comparison."

"We've started the cheek swab process for those who volunteer." Goose bumps rose on Ellie's arms. *The morgue is extra frosty today.* Wrapping her hands over her elbows, she tried not to shiver. "I'm heading back to the precinct after this. I'll check with Lancaster and get a status update on those for you."

"Good, good. Now that that's out of the way..." Doctor Faizal joined Ellie beside Bernard's body. "I came across something while digging into this guy. Cause of death is pretty straightforward. Blunt force trauma to the skull, right?"

Ellie nodded.

The M.E.'s finger hovered above the body, pointing as she spoke. "Damage to the spine, the torso. Ruptured organs. All consistent with a fall from his twelfth-story apartment onto the roof of a car. You agree?"

Again, Ellie nodded.

Doctor Faizal frowned and shook her head. "But this is a big guy. And you suggested he hadn't jumped on his own accord. So I wondered how another person could have thrown this giant from the balcony or even forced him to jump at all. Bernard could've easily taken down three men on his own."

Ellie agreed with her logic. He'd been in the correct profession. Bernard's bulging body was built for security detail. Or a bouncer at a club.

"I took a closer look and found this." The M.E. retrieved a

small magnifying glass from the pocket of her lab coat, crouched over the body, and stretched the skin at the side of Bernard's neck. She waved her finger at a spot near the point where his neck met his trapezius muscle. "Here. There's a puncture wound. Very tiny. Easy to overlook."

She angled the magnifying glass to offer Ellie a better view.

An almost invisible prick materialized through the glass. Ellie sucked in a breath and made a mental note to send forensics to Bernard's apartment pronto. *That's how the killer tossed Bernard over. A drug.*

Doctor Faizal leaned back and returned the magnifying glass to her pocket. "The tox screen came back positive for a paralytic called Vecuronium bromide."

"That sounds nasty." A phantom metallic taste formed at the back of Ellie's mouth. Was this what the killer used on her brother?

"Oh, it most certainly is. The drug is part of a cocktail used for lethal injections and can be in either powder form or injected straight into a person's vein. This drug is also given right before anesthesia in hospital situations. Anyone given the correct amount of the formula would experience short-term paralysis," the M.E. waved her hand over the table, "like Bernard here. A person who succeeded in pumping Bernard with a dose of this would have no trouble forcing him over the balcony. Gravity would take care of the rest."

Ellie shivered, but not because of the temperature. The idea of not being able to move her body while someone tossed her to her death terrified her. Her mind drifted to her visit to the Coastline Inn, where she'd slipped on the rocks. For a brief moment, she'd lost control of her limbs. If not for Lancaster, she would've fallen into the rushing river and been swept away by the currents.

"Would it be easy to get this stuff? Like on the black market?" Ellie peered at the teeny-tiny puncture on Bernard's neck. Without the magnifying glass, the hole vanished into his skin once again.

Did someone dump the drug into Dan's drink at the club?

Her heartbeat quickened. "And, if a lethal dose were injected in a person, is there an antidote?"

The M.E. puckered her lips and angled her head. "I imagine something like neostigmine or sugammadex could reverse the effects. As far as the black market, it's not easy to locate. In fact, I was shocked to even find the drug in this guy's system."

Could this be the information the doctors need to cure Dan?

Ellie swallowed, her throat as dry as the Sahara. "So the person who injected him had to know where to look to purchase some?" She stared down at Bernard's body.

"Oh, yes." Doctor Faizal inhaled and nodded. "And if they didn't intend to kill the target, they'd need to know how to dose the other person correctly. Vecuronium bromide is a high-alert medication. Used incorrectly, it can cause significant harm."

Ellie directed her gaze at Monique's body. "What about her? Was the drug used on her too?"

"No." The M.E. sighed and crossed her arms. "Poor Monique was just a tiny woman overpowered by someone larger than her."

"Have you gotten the victim we discovered this morning? Kira Long?"

"I have, but she's in storage until I've finished with Bernard. Although, her cause of death appears to be several stab wounds. You want me to test her for the drug too?"

"Yes, please."

"Will do." Doctor Faizal rolled her neck, causing it to pop.

"That's all I've got for now. Get me those cheek swabs, and I'll have more information for you."

"Sounds like a plan." Ellie rushed to the door. "Until next time."

The fluorescent lights in the small area outside the autopsy room purred and flickered as Ellie snapped off the gloves, slipped off the gown, and jiggled the booties off her shoes. She dropped the items into a waste container.

A call to her mother went straight to voicemail, and an automated message relayed that the mailbox was full. Ellie bit the inside of her cheek. *I can't leave a message, and this is too important to hope Mom's checking her texts.*

She redialed the number. Again, the call went to the automatic message. Ellie exhaled, the puff of air sending loose strands of her hair flying above her head. Calls to her father and Blake went unanswered too.

Fine. I'll just keep trying on my way to the precinct.

Exiting into the hallway, she compared the three deaths.

Monique was shoved off a balcony, and Bernard was drugged and shoved off a balcony. As far as the M.O. was concerned, their deaths were consistent.

The killer changed tactics with Kira. Her death was violent and messy. Not like the others. The killer was pissed when he caught her. Angrier than he'd been at his other two victims.

Kira had been keeping secrets. *Did those secrets get her killed?* Ellie wasn't sure. The brutal attack seemed extra personal, though. Like payback.

But for what?

28

When Ellie returned from the morgue, the precinct bustled with activity. Silently cursing the tinny on-hold music the hospital used, she stepped through the doors as groups of people headed out to the parking lot. She could have driven to the hospital and searched every room in the time it was taking the operator to locate the damn doctor.

Inside, she passed detectives at their desks slurping noodles and chomping on hoagie sandwiches. Upon entering the kitchen, she spotted two women snacking on salads in the adjoining break room.

She checked her watch. *Is it lunchtime already?* Emptiness filled her belly like a lead ball. With all the commotion that morning, she'd never eaten breakfast. She flipped through the takeout menus in the kitchen before a box of stale doughnuts on the counter captured her eye.

Maybe I'll just grab one of those and a coffee.

Her stomach panged in protest.

Ignoring her ravenous appetite, Ellie poured herself a cup of coffee. After wasting precious minutes searching the cabinets for more sugar packets, she spied the empty box that once held them resting at the top of the trash bin. *In that case, I'll take two doughnuts.* Ellie popped two glazed circles onto a napkin, grabbed her drink, and made her way toward the bullpen, the on-hold music still playing in her ear.

As she passed Stoddard's office, which, minutes before, was empty, movement in her periphery grabbed her attention. She jerked her head and stopped short, her shoe skidding on the tile. The doughnuts threatened to jump ship, but she managed to rescue them before it was too late. Frazzled, she kept her eyes trained on the scene in Stoddard's office.

Lancaster was in a deep conversation with Stoddard. They turned and glanced in Ellie's direction through the large window.

Why do I feel like I've just been caught in the crosshairs?

Ellie continued to her desk, conscious of the two sets of eyes stalking her every move.

She nearly jumped when a voice spoke in her ear. "University Medical Center, how may I direct your—"

The line went dead.

Staring at her phone in disbelief, Ellie tossed her bag into a drawer and slammed her makeshift lunch down on her desk. She was about to call the hospital back when Lancaster appeared in front of her desk.

"Good afternoon. I'm gonna go out on a limb and guess you've already visited Kira's place without me." The words rolled off his tongue like dew on an early morning leaf. "You're welcome for doing all of the legwork for you with the warrant."

What was that about? Ellie's cheeks burned at being called out for leaving him behind. Again. *If he isn't beating around the bush, then neither am I.* She lifted her chin. "The secret conference with Stoddard? Were you discussing me?"

He stiffened. "You know, not everything is about you. She

and I were discussing details of the case. I need someone to bounce ideas off of. It's not like you're around, the way you keep going off on your own. Thanks for the invite to Kira's apartment, by the way. Highlighter-yellow sticky notes are so formal."

"I work fine on my own." She tapped out a message for her mother to call her as soon as possible. "I don't need a babysitter. I'm here now. Let's focus on the case."

"Okay. Truce." Lancaster raised his palms. "I'm glad you came in. We're having some good luck with the cheek swabs." He pointed to a small conference room where a heavyset man with slicked-back blond hair perched on an office chair, his mouth wide open.

Even as Ellie followed Lancaster's arm with her gaze, suspicion prickled along her scalp. Defensiveness when she asked about his discussion with Stoddard. Immediately attacking her behavior. Offering a truce with no pushback.

Nothing added up here. Or it did.

Lancaster was hiding something.

"Really? That's awesome." *Doctor Faizal will be thrilled.* Ellie hesitated, considering whether to mention the drug in the security guard's system to Lancaster. She decided against sharing the information and instead smiled at him. "Thank you for taking the lead on that. I spoke to the M.E. The confirmed cause of death is the twelve-story fall."

Although the Vecuronium bromide would show up in the autopsy report, not mentioning the presence of a drug might buy her some time to figure out what was going on. Besides, having observed the way Lancaster operated over the past few days, she doubted he'd go beyond her word to verify the details himself.

After all, according to his way of thinking, that would just be a waste of time.

"Well, that's what we expected, right?" His brown eyes

softened. "How's your brother doing? Doctors find anything yet?"

You've never asked before. A sliver of mistrust lodged itself inside Ellie's rib cage as she noted Lancaster's further misdirection tactic of swinging hard in the other direction toward empathy.

Still, Ellie swallowed hard, trying to keep the nerves at bay. *Vecuronium bromide is a high-alert medication. Used incorrectly, it can cause significant harm.* Doctor Faizal's discovery of the drug in Bernard Cookson's body could be the key to saving her brother. Or another dead end. *Either way, the doctors should be told to look for traces.*

"No changes, but I do need to check on him." She pulled out the phone in her back pocket and stared at the screen. Still no messages or calls from her mother. Or her dad. Or anyone.

"Sure." Lancaster glanced back at Stoddard's office. "Real quick, though. I've been reviewing those bank records. Nothing unusual has turned up."

Nothing unusual?

Given the statement she'd unearthed in Kira's apartment, plenty unusual should've turned up.

"Thanks for the update." Ellie held back mention of Kira's lavish expenses and consulting deposits from Delecroix Logistics. Though Lancaster seemed to be offering an olive branch regarding their partnership, she trusted him even less now than she did before. She held her phone in the air. "Keep up the good work. I'm going to step outside and call my mom."

She slid out from behind her desk and scooted into the hall for privacy. The air conditioning rattled on above her.

Her mother picked up immediately. "Ellie? I'm sorry I missed your calls. We were discussing options with the doctors."

"How's Dan doing? Any change?"

An exhausted sigh drifted into Ellie's ear. "No. No updates. No change. One of my friends suggested we look into finding a specialist at another facility, maybe even another state. Or country. At this point, I'm not sure what to do."

"I'll tell you what to do. Get out a pen and piece of paper." Ellie nodded at another detective heading into the community room.

"Pen and paper? What for?"

Ellie didn't want to tell her mom the details, that Doctor Faizal had indicated the drug in Bernard Cookson's system could be fatal if misused. The M.E. had also mentioned a powdered form of the high-alert medication. Perfect for dumping into a distracted person's glass at a noisy club.

"Actually, I'll text you the spelling, but what I need you to do is tell the doctor to check for Vecuronium bromide. It's not something they normally look for." She started the text even as she spoke.

"Verco…" Her mother paused. "What's this about, Ellie?"

Ellie hit send on the message. "Mom, please, just have the doctors check. It's important."

"All right, all right. I got the text."

Please, Mom. Get that to the doctors ASAP.

29

Clay's grin fell when he stepped into the bullpen on the precinct's second floor and found Ellie's desk empty. *Okay, I know she's here. The woman eats, sleeps, and breathes her job.*

The fast-food bag hooked under his arm scorched his skin. He switched the bag to his other elbow and wandered past the handful of detectives milling around at their desks. Ellie wasn't in the kitchen or break room either. He returned the fast-food bag to the original arm and continued down the hallway.

She's got to be here somewhere.

He found her in a conference room beside the elevator to the basement. Roughly the size of a standard closet, there was only space for a large table and a couple skinny chairs. Why she'd chosen to set up shop in such a cramped area baffled him.

I can barely breathe in here, let alone think.

Puffs of Ellie's red hair curled over her eyebrows. Her head dipped toward her laptop screen. She was so engrossed in her work, she didn't notice him approach.

Clay rapped on the door. "I'm looking for this

department's star detective. About this high, with the greenest eyes I've ever seen." He leveled his hand to his nose and skirted around the oversize table.

Ellie smiled. "What are you doing here?" Her grin widened when she spied the bag of cheeseburgers.

Clay handed her the goods and sat on the edge of the table, his tan cargo shorts riding up his thigh. Producing an unopened bottle of water from one pocket, he placed the beverage in front of Ellie. "I couldn't stand the thought of you being here, all alone, slowly wasting away as you jumped back into your first case since your suspension."

Ellie beamed. "And you brought me lunch. Thank you. You're a godsend. I was starving."

"Looks like I got here just in time." He frowned at the napkin beside her topped with doughnut crumbles. "I also needed to check on some things for my case."

She popped a glistening fry into her mouth, crunching it between her teeth. "The missing-kids case?"

"Yeah. I want to check out a few files in the cold case archives. LaPierre might be at the very center of the child-trafficking ring I'm investigating. That doesn't sit well with me." He snuck a loose fry from the bag.

"I'd imagine not." She held the paper cup out to him. "Haven't you eaten either? We can share."

Clay licked the salt and grease off his fingers. "No, I'm good. I'm just peckish." He chuckled before changing the subject. "Where's your partner?"

Ellie reached for the water bottle and unscrewed the cap. A faint *crack* whispered through the room as the seal broke. "He's taking a late lunch." She exhaled, pausing for dramatic effect. "With Stoddard."

"That's odd."

Lead Detective Stoddard was an expert at keeping boundaries. At least, according to what Ellie had told him and what he'd observed with his own eyes. Heading out for a lunch date with a detective in her charge was out of character for the usually standoffish woman.

"Yes, it is. Just imagining what they're discussing makes me nervous. I find their camaraderie very suspicious." She tore into the cheeseburger like she'd been starved for weeks. A look of pure ecstasy bloomed over her face, and she lifted her fist to cover her mouth as she spoke through her food. "But it gets Lancaster out of my hair, so I'm not going to complain too much."

"That's my girl." Clay gestured to the stack of papers next to her laptop. "Is that all for the LaPierre case?"

"Yes. Bank records. Although, the printing on these pages is so tiny, I might go blind staring at them." Ketchup oozed from the corner of Ellie's mouth. Her lips curved into a smile when he reached over and softly swiped away the condiment splatter with the tip of his knuckle.

Laughter broke out in the hallway. A couple of uniformed officers passed by the door, chattering about a baseball game. After a *ding* echoed through the hall, their conversation disappeared behind the *whoosh* of the elevator doors.

Clay wiped the ketchup off his finger with a napkin before holding a bank statement up and perusing the information. Ellie was right. The transactions for LaPierre's services and fees crossed the page like minuscule ants on the way to a picnic. "If it's any help, I can confirm that Delecroix Logistics is a primary funding source for the LaPierre Foundation. In fact, our team has pinpointed several different donations made to LaPierre through a ton of dummy corporations. All of them link back to Delecroix."

Ellie sank back into her chair. "Yeah, that's super shady. Why such secrecy?"

"Exactly. Companies love getting tax breaks, and charitable donations are typically tax deductible. So the fact that a company would choose to mask their donations beneath a shell corporation is curious." He set the sheet back on the table and pointed at a second stack of papers next to the first. "What are those?"

"Kira Long's bank records. Wanna take a peek? They're curious too." Ellie patted the chair next to her.

Clay dropped into the seat and tugged the top sheet from the stack. Payments to Delecroix hid behind charges at luxury shopping sites and fancy restaurants. He scratched his chin.

Consulting fees? What guidance would Kira Long be providing to Delecroix?

He set the paper back on top of the stack. "This case keeps getting stranger and stranger."

Ellie twirled a loose strand of hair around her finger and wrapped the tendril over her ear. "Tell me about it. Why are LaPierre and Delecroix so linked? One's a charitable foundation and the other's a logistics firm. And how on earth does Kira factor into all of it?"

"Or Quint Bannister. As one of LaPierre's former kids, he's definitely tied into this somehow." Clay stole another fry and popped it into his mouth. Bannister's record was far from clean, but he came off as more of a slimeball than a murderer. He also had no real motive for the crimes. "Although, he doesn't appear to be part of the group lodging the abuse allegations against LaPierre. Not the one we received for our child-trafficking case."

"Funny you mention Quint. I want to chat with Donna Montague again. Odds are he'll be lurking around her somewhere. Maybe I can question them at the same time. First the reward, and now the confirmation that Quint was a LaPierre recipient. It's weird, right?" Ellie's green eyes settled on Clay.

"I'm not sure I follow you."

A frown marred her lightly freckled face. "Earlier in the case, I joked with Lancaster that Donna set up the reward because she killed Monique and wanted to make the investigation difficult for us, but what if she really *is* trying to sabotage the investigation because Quint's involved? You know, offer that huge reward to muck up our chances of singling him out?"

"Anything's possible at this point. You planning to head out and talk to her soon?"

There were still hours of daylight left to burn. If they headed out now, they could take in a matinee and catch an early dinner afterward. *Please say no. Say you'd rather close up shop for the day and laze away the rest of the day with me.*

Ellie glanced at the large, old-school clock on the wall. "Lancaster's still out to lunch with our boss. He'll be pissed if I leave him out of another interview. But…I don't want to wait on this. So yes, I'm going now." Shrugging, she closed her laptop.

Clay stood and moved closer to her. "Just be careful. You might have a serial killer on your hands. If Quint is your guy, he's dangerous, and Donna's using her power and money to enable him."

Ellie rose from her chair and rested her hand on his chest. "Well, if I do have a serial killer on my hands, you keep yourself at a distance. Hands off, okay? This is my collar first."

"Don't hold your breath." Clay laughed, but the sound rang hollow.

30

A phone call to the Montague estate informed Ellie that Donna was out. Undeterred, she headed to Donna's other listed residence, a million-dollar home nestled within the Ansonborough neighborhood of Charleston's Historic District.

This area, known for its rich history, boasted several houses dating back to the mid-1800s. A devastating fire in 1838 had razed much of the neighborhood, leading to a wave of brick reconstruction—a condition set by city officials for establishing a fund to rebuild.

Ellie parked her SUV on the street and hopped out onto a sidewalk lined with palmetto and oak trees. Donna's house boasted a mixture of aged brick and painted white wood, which Ellie guessed was the original structure. The location on the north side of Ansonborough, less than a half mile from the Cooper River, would've spared the home from the fire.

A couple cars sat off to one side of the building, in front of another house set farther back from the road. Ellie wandered to the other side of the home and peered over the wrought iron privacy fence. The street door connected to an open-air porch that ran along the side of the home and led to the main entrance. At the back corner of the property, she glimpsed a colorful garden's lush foliage.

Stepping back to the street door, she rang the bell. A briny breeze from the nearby harbor scuttled past. Down the road, a group of people chatted as they snapped photos and enjoyed the beautiful afternoon. The sun dappled through the tree leaves and onto the sidewalk, the light at the coveted golden hour photographers loved to work in. Not too harsh, not too bright.

After a moment, Ellie rang the bell again and rapped against the door. *C'mon, Donna. Be here.* Behind the door, another one slammed, and feet shuffled along the porch.

As the door edged open, Donna's nose and one eye peeked out. She released a loud huff once she realized her visitor was Ellie. "What are you doing here? I assumed we'd finished our business." The woman's cheeks burned bright red, and she jerked the door open wider. When she stepped forward, the breeze picked up again and rustled the kimono she wore over a satin gown with spaghetti straps.

A blur materialized over Donna's shoulder. Ellie leaned over to get a better view and pursed her lips.

It was Quint Bannister, clad in no more than a thin bathrobe. He gnawed on a thick slice of bacon, baring his teeth with each bite. He raised one of his dark eyebrows and slowly licked grease from his lips while locking eyes with Ellie.

Donna glanced back with a raspy sigh. "Quint, I told you to stay in the house." She raked her fingers through her mussed white-blond hair.

Stopping, he shrugged and leaned his shoulder against the

exterior wall. As he lounged, he picked bits of bacon out of his teeth, regarding the two women with the nonchalance of a bored child. Another breeze brought the edges of his robe dangerously close to wardrobe-malfunction territory.

"Now isn't the best time." Donna dismissed Ellie with a twiglike arm, pushing her body against the door until the barrier was half closed. "Whatever it is, you'll need to call my secretary and schedule an appointment."

Ellie stuck her foot between the door and frame to prevent Donna from shutting her out. "I'm afraid this can't wait. I'll only take a few minutes of your time. Promise."

Donna lifted her chin and raised a brow. "Do I need to call my lawyer?"

"That's up to you. I just want to have a friendly conversation. If you haven't done anything wrong in relation to Monique LaPierre's case, we shouldn't have an issue."

Donna sighed like a petulant teenager. After reopening the door, she gestured to the porch. "Fine. We might as well take this inside and stop giving the neighbors a free show."

Ellie scooted through the door and followed Donna down the enclosed porch. Quint ogled them from his spot against the wall. As they passed by him, he sucked on his bottom lip and winked at Ellie, the odor of onions even stronger than the last time they met.

The sweet doughnuts, savory cheeseburger, and fries from earlier swirled in Ellie's stomach and surged up her throat. She gulped the unholy concoction back down.

The wooden floorboards creaked as Quint's bare feet padded behind them. At the center of the porch, Donna opened a yellowish-brown door surrounded by square glass panels and stepped inside. "I'll give you ten minutes. No more."

"Fine by me."

Ellie strode into a bright foyer lit by a large window from the floor above. Two arched doorways flanked a rounded staircase. Donna motioned for her to follow through the one on the right.

The arch led Ellie into a sitting room that resembled an interior design photo on a glossy magazine cover. Pretty, but not lived in.

Crisp, white crown molding bordered narrow walls painted a cold, pale blue. A single cream-colored cabinet with faded books on open shelves lurked in a back corner. The other corner harbored a large, similarly colored fireplace decked in gilded frames. An abstract artwork of bright yellow and orange brushstrokes—the single item with any true color in the room—spanned the largest wall behind a thick-cushioned couch.

Ellie scooted between a couple of light-gray armchairs to the fireplace. The hardwood floor groaned beneath her shoes, encouraging her to take lighter steps. Moving closer to the back of the room, she spotted a hefty layer of dust settling into the crevices of the books in the cabinet and the frames on the mantel.

A musty scent that'd invaded her nostrils when she first entered worked its way deeper into her lungs. *This entire room reeks of neglect.* A stark contrast to Melody Long's warm, cluttered living room.

Donna slunk to an armchair and took a seat. Tiny dust mites shot from the flattened cushion and scrambled around a streak of late afternoon sunlight breaking through the lace curtains covering the room's only window.

Quint sprawled out on the couch, his robe's slit just managing to close, narrowly preserving his decency. Reaching under the terrycloth, he gave his balls a good scratch before producing another slice of fried, salt-cured pork from his robe pocket. His teeth ripped into the meat.

How many pieces of bacon does he have in that pocket?

Ellie gulped down her disgust and decided she didn't want to know.

Donna side-eyed Quint before tossing her irritated gaze Ellie's way. "So? What's so important that you had to invade my quiet Thursday afternoon?"

To avoid sitting, Ellie scrutinized the pictures crowding the mantel. Many showcased Donna standing next to celebrities and politicians. None resembled family photos.

She sighed. *Like I'm any better. My apartment doesn't have much in the way of photos either.* A problem she planned to rectify the minute she finished this case. Dozens of photos languished on her phone, begging to be printed. After she acquired a few frames, she'd be one step closer to the happy haven of a comfier home.

Ellie turned and directed her attention to Quint first, then Donna. "I thought you were married."

Quint cackled and gnawed at his bacon slice.

Donna straightened in her seat. Clearing her throat, she glared at Ellie. "Not that it's any of your business, but I am. My husband and I have an...an understanding."

"So he's perfectly fine with..." Ellie gestured toward Quint, "this?"

Donna crossed her arms. "Again, not your business."

Fair enough. Okay, I'll get to the point.

Ellie tilted her head. "You offered a huge reward for information regarding Monique's murder. Why not for Kira Long?"

Donna scoffed and crossed her legs. "Why on earth would I? It's not a big mystery or anything. I didn't really know anything about the woman, except that she was desperate to be one of us."

Ellie shifted to Quint. "What about you? Did you know Kira Long?"

"Yep." He tossed his last crumble of bacon into his mouth and grinned. When he leaned forward, the top portion of his robe sprang open to reveal his hairy chest. "I knew her *real* well."

Ellie's skin crawled at the way he lingered on the word. "How so?"

His eyes slowly roamed over her body. "I was a LaPierre recipient awhile back."

The blasé way he responded to her questions boiled her blood. *Is he even taking any of this seriously?*

"Why? What trouble were you in?"

He shrugged and dropped his greasy hands between his knees. "Stealing. Fighting. The usual LaPierre recipient stuff."

"Did you have any animosity toward the foundation? A grudge?"

His back straightened, and his face lost all humor as he shook his head. For the first time since she'd crossed paths with him, Quint Bannister appeared dead serious. "They saved me, honestly. I was headed down a bad path when LaPierre found me. That place saved my life. Mostly because Monique and Kira saw something in me I didn't know existed. Decency. They changed my life for the better. If I'd never met them, I wouldn't be here today. I know that for certain."

Donna massaged her temples. "All that good enough for you, Detective Kline? Quint wouldn't hurt a fly now. Unless it asked him to." The sultry stare Donna shot Quint made Ellie cringe.

"No. We aren't quite finished. Where were you last night?" She looked back and forth between Donna and Quint. "Both of you."

They responded in unison. "Together."

"Where?" Ellie wasn't sure she wanted to know the answer.

"At a restaurant. Rosarito's, across town. My name should be on the reservation list. I could even provide a credit card transaction to confirm." Donna wiggled in her seat.

"Can you do that right now?"

Donna shook her head. "I don't have it with me."

Gritting her teeth, Ellie reached into her back pocket and pulled out a business card. "I'll take you up on that offer. Forward the receipt to me." She walked over to the armchair and handed Donna the card.

"Are we done?" Donna snatched it from her fingertips. Her gaze drifted back to Quint and her lips parted, the tip of her tongue pushing against the corner of her wrinkled mouth. "Quint and I were...all tied up in something when you dropped by."

Gross.

Ellie spun on her heel and headed for the foyer, pausing before turning back. "Don't forget to email that information to me. ASAP."

Donna only offered a dismissive wave, already rising from her seat and sashaying toward a reclining Quint. With a grin, he rested his head against the back of the couch. A third slice of bacon poked out from his robe pocket.

Good god.

Hustling, Ellie rushed out of the house and back to the safety of her SUV. She couldn't get back to the precinct fast enough as she pulled away from the curb.

I wonder if Mom's found out anything about that drug yet? She picked her phone back up and tapped the device against her chin, thinking as she drove. *Although, Mom would've called if anything had happened since we last spoke.*

She hesitated, torn over bothering her parents. If they were finally getting some rest, food, or information from the doctors, she didn't want to distract them.

Her phone buzzed. Startled, she jumped in her seat. When she answered, Lancaster's annoyed voice greeted her.

"Look, I don't know where you've run off to by yourself again, but I got access to Kira's phone records. You won't believe what I've found…"

31

An unholy odor of wet socks and boiled cabbage permeated the air as Ellie passed the men's locker room at the precinct. Pressing her back against the wall, she sidestepped a janitor mopping up a brown stain in the hallway. The heel of her shoe slid on a wet spot, and she almost flew into a yellow *caution* sign a couple feet away.

Heat rushed to her face. She peered around to see if anyone witnessed her Klutz of the Year performance. Thankfully, the only person within eyeshot—the janitor—seemed too lost in his own thoughts to even notice her.

The wretched reek weakened the closer she got to the community room. As she passed by, she peeked into Stoddard's office. The lead detective wasn't there and, judging from the darkness inside, didn't plan on returning until tomorrow.

Ellie relaxed. No Stoddard meant no intrusive questions to evade. Or reminders that she was saddled with a partner.

Speaking of...

Lancaster's beefy form came into view once she rounded the corner. Light-yellow earbuds protruded from his ears as he hunched over his laptop, his fingers *clacking* away on the keyboard. A limp suit jacket hung on the back of his chair.

Her eyes shot back to Stoddard's empty office. *What were you two conspiring about earlier this afternoon?* The mere memory of stumbling upon them, deep in a private conversation, raised Ellie's blood pressure.

I might not follow the rules and regs, but I get results. Don't I?

She'd made mistakes in a few of her most recent cases. Not following proper police procedure. Defying her superiors. Even coercing her loved ones into helping her skirt the law.

Ignoring her natural instincts to rush off on her own and save the day was difficult, but Ellie was working hard to be more conscious of how her actions and decisions affected the people around her.

So damn hard.

Her blood heated at the idea that Stoddard and Lancaster were discussing some new faux pas she'd committed. *I've followed Stoddard's rules. I've been a team player.* She pressed her lips together.

Mostly.

As nagging paranoia seeped into her mind, Ellie inhaled a deep breath and rolled her neck, counting back from ten in her head. A trick her therapist taught her to relieve tension. Her shoulders relaxed.

Whatever those two were discussing, I can't worry about it now.

She strode forward, knocking on Lancaster's desk when she reached her partner.

He jerked his head up before pushing back his chair and pulling an earbud from his ear. "Wow. I didn't expect you back so quick."

Ellie strolled to her own desk and set her bag down. "You sounded urgent on the phone. What's going on?"

Lancaster rolled the chair to his desk before pulling a printout from a manila folder and waving the sheet. "Here."

Wrinkling her brow, Ellie accepted the paper. "What am I looking at?"

"I've been tracing the known numbers in Kira Long's phone records. Haven't gotten too far, but I figured this would interest you. The number on top is the last number she dialed. The call we saw in the security footage."

Her gaze fixated on a line circled in pink highlighter at the top of the page. "Prescott, Lester, and Faucett?"

The bank statement she'd discovered in Kira's apartment showed that the woman paid for *PLF Legal Services*, but Ellie didn't connect the dots right away. *PLF. Prescott, Lester, and Faucett, one of the most distinguished and pricey law firms in Charleston.*

"You familiar with them?" Lancaster raised an eyebrow and tilted his head.

She nodded as she studied the page. "Yeah. Prescott, Lester, and Faucett, LLC is a law firm based here in Charleston. Super prestigious. The firm's clientele is a good chunk of upper-class elites in and around the city."

Why would Kira call a law firm after ten p.m.? More importantly, who did she speak with at that law firm so late at night? Ellie placed the paper on Lancaster's desk.

He scribbled an asterisk next to the circled information. "I'll give them a call tomorrow. Maybe Kira was a client."

Ellie considered Kira's bare-bones apartment, sparsely decorated with a few expensive furniture pieces. "My guess is no. I doubt she could afford their services."

Lancaster shrugged. "I figure it's a long shot on getting much information from them anyway. In my experience, lawyers cling to their client-attorney privilege. We'll probably need a warrant at some point."

"I'll trust you to stay on top of that." A stiff ache settled into Ellie's right ankle. She shifted her weight to her left hip. "What's your take on Quint Bannister? My skin wants to crawl away every time I interact with him."

Lancaster chuckled. "Don't really have one, since I haven't met the guy personally, but I'll trust your word."

"I can't get an angle on him. He's the perfect potential suspect. He's got a history, he's brazen and egotistical, and he's creepy as hell. He also had nothing but good things to say about LaPierre. Especially Monique and Kira. And I can't place him anywhere near the mayor's fundraiser the night of Monique's murder."

A layer of smarm still coated Ellie from her recent interaction with Donna Montague and Quint. She tried to shake away the lingering disgust snaking up her spine.

"Join the club. Dude's suspect gold." Lancaster grunted and scratched the back of his bald head. "Though, if two people were murdered, would you admit how much you really hated them? Especially if you wanted the cops to stop looking your way?"

"Fair point." Ellie crossed her arms. "There's also his odd relationship with Donna Montague. Could she have coaxed Quint into doing her dirty work?"

"My thought? No. The person who killed Kira was pissed as hell at her. If Quint was simply doing Donna's bidding, he wouldn't have gotten so personal with the murder."

Her shoulders sagged. "Another good point."

The more she considered Donna and Quint, the less she viewed them as suspects. Donna cut her enemies down with rude remarks, and murder would require too much effort for someone as lazy as Quint.

And just like that, I'm back to square one.

She pointed at the manila file on Lancaster's desk. "Anything else pop up on the phone records besides the law firm?"

He shook his head. "Nada. Unless you count a lack of phone calls to her mother as dubious. Me, I call my mama every day to chew the fat. She's in a nursing home near West Ashley. Got Alzheimer's. On a good day, she recognizes my voice, but she usually thinks I'm a nice stranger checking on her. Or I'm my dad, who passed thirty years back."

For the first time, Ellie noticed the wrinkles swimming on Lancaster's forehead and the hint of gray in his five o'clock shadow.

He probably knows a ton about me. Why haven't I bothered to learn anything about him?

"Is it difficult? Chewing the fat when she doesn't remember you?"

Ellie's heart squeezed. Could she look into her own mother's eyes knowing her mother only saw a stranger?

"You think I don't know you eat when you're stressed? At least, more than you usually scarf down in a sitting."

Her mother's words flittered into her mind and nipped at her heart. Thinking that one—or even both—of her parents could someday forget her gutted her.

"Yeah." Lancaster raised large, chestnut-brown eyes to meet her gaze. The precinct's harsh fluorescent lighting glistened in his pupils. "Most days, it's damn hard. Especially on Sundays, when I visit her at the home and take her out for lunch. If she's willing to go, that is. But I got to maintain that connection with her."

Ellie offered him a sad smile. "Sounds like you're doing the best you can in the situation."

He cleared his throat and shifted back to his laptop. "I try, but as far as the phone records go, nothing else stuck out to me."

She nodded, accepting his cue to end their personal conversation. "Okay, let me know if that changes." Ellie shuffled over to her desk, pausing when she sat in her chair to peek at the other detective.

Maybe the discussion with Stoddard really wasn't about her.

Lancaster's sad story anchored into her heart and refused to abate. She rubbed the back of her neck, feeling guilty for the way she'd treated him yesterday. Maybe her skepticism and mistrust had led her to imagine that Lancaster was manipulating her earlier.

I need to get my mind on something else.

The best distraction? Work.

Picking up her phone, she dialed the number for the medical examiner's office. With Doctor Faizal out, the call was transferred to a young male assistant Ellie had met once or twice in passing.

After a brief greeting, she jumped right in with her question. "Any new information on Kira Long?"

"Can't help you much. The autopsy's scheduled for tomorrow afternoon." He sneezed on the other end of the line. "Excuse me. Spring cold."

"Bless you."

"Thanks." Tissue rustled as the assistant blew his nose. "I can tell you the initial postmortem shows significant internal trauma due to a sharp-edged instrument. Nothing too mysterious."

"What about defensive wounds? Did she fight?"

"No. Not much in the way of defensive wounds."

With a sigh, Ellie requested that Doctor Faizal call her the minute she completed the autopsy and hung up.

She'd learned one thing. Her instincts from when she and Lancaster had viewed the security footage in the parking garage were spot-on. Kira hadn't expected the ambush. She knew her attacker and didn't view them as a threat.

Ellie's thoughts returned to Quint Bannister. He'd admitted to knowing Kira *"real well."* The insinuation of their intimacy might have been a catalyst for the brutality of the attack.

He had a history with LaPierre, too, and a shaky—at best—alibi. Even if Donna Montague emailed Ellie the restaurant receipt from her Wednesday night rendezvous with Quint, the information would only prove Donna was there. Or rather, her credit card.

Still, Ellie maintained Quint was too lazy to commit murder without a powerful incentive. *So think about motive. What could his motive be to kill Monique?*

She frowned. *The baby.*

If Donna found out he'd impregnated one of her peers, she might be livid enough to cut him off from his special privileges. No more sex, no more luxurious gifts, no more living the high life. That might be incentive enough to get a person like Quint off his ass for murder.

Priority number one...get Quint in for a cheek swab. What about Kira, though? Did she know about the baby and try to blackmail him?

Possibly. Although, with Kira, there were so many possibilities and unknown factors. She was involved in shady practices, of that Ellie was certain. The question was, what *type* of shady practices?

The pieces refused to fit neatly together. She sensed the answer hovering right in front of her, just beyond her grasp. *I'm missing something.*

Ellie massaged her temples. When her stomach growled, she peeked at her watch. *It's late.*

Rising from her chair, she grabbed her bag and sashayed out of the police department. Her limbs were stiff, and her belly was empty. She'd provided more than enough of her blood, sweat, and tears to the Charleston PD for the day.

Time to go home, eat something, and salvage what little time I have left this evening by spending the night with Bethany.

Outside, the constant cry of tree frogs blasted her ears, and dark clouds mingled with the fading blue sky. Patches of dying sunlight pooled across the parking lot. Despite the heavy heat and humidity settling on top of her, a sudden chill covered Ellie's body. The tiny hairs on her arms shot to attention.

She paused in the empty space beside her SUV and rubbed a hand up and down her arm. Swirling around, she peered beyond a row of trees into a half-filled parking lot across from the precinct. The setting sun bounced off the vehicles' windshields, preventing her from seeing if any of the cars were occupied. A breeze rustled the leaves, but the rest of the parking lot remained still.

This case is rattling my nerves. Nothing some quality time with Beth and a good night's sleep can't fix.

With one final glance at the other parking lot, Ellie hopped into her SUV and headed home.

32

As Bethany shoveled the remaining forkful of syrup-drenched pancakes between her sticky lips, she hummed a happy tune while she chewed. Ellie chuckled as the little girl reached for a glass of pulpy orange juice and finished the beverage off. Soft sunlight poured in from the clear balcony door, shimmering off the silver fork resting on Bethany's now-empty dish.

"I take it your breakfast was good?" Ellie was glad they tasted better than they looked. An expert pancake flipper she was not.

"Oh, yeah." Bethany patted her belly. "I'm super full."

Ellie laughed and stacked Bethany's gooey plate onto her own. She dropped their forks on top and headed into the kitchen to rinse the dishes.

When her phone vibrated on the table, Bethany snatched the device up first and checked the screen. "It's Nana Helen." Her wide eyes met Ellie's.

Over the past few days, every time her mother called, a knot had formed in Ellie's chest. One that grew larger and larger each day. She'd been holding tight to the adage that no news was good news. Every time her phone buzzed, she hesitated to pick up.

Bethany held the phone out. "Aren't you going to answer?"

Rushing over, Ellie tapped a button on the screen and lifted the device to her ear. If the news was bad, she didn't want Bethany to overhear. "Hey, Mom."

"He's awake!"

Ellie wilted into the closest chair and nearly wept with relief. "He is? Is he coherent? How does he sound?"

Her mother's giggles bounced into Ellie's heart. The delirious mood could only mean one thing.

Dan's going to be okay.

"Come see for yourself." A happy sigh exuded from the receiver. "Oh, Ellie, I'm so grateful. Hurry over, okay?"

Ellie ended the call and released a breath from deep inside her soul. She turned to Bethany. "Uncle Dan's going to be okay."

A huge grin lit the little girl's face. "Does this mean he can go home soon?"

"Hopefully. All I know is that he's up." Ellie hopped out of the chair and snatched the syrup bottle and tub of butter from the table. "Let's get this mess cleaned up so we can get you to school."

❈

A beaming crowd of Klines greeted Ellie in the waiting room at the university medical center. She scurried over to her father and threw her arms around him, overcome with relief when he gripped her tight.

When they pulled apart, tears stained his face. He touched her cheek. "I'm fine, really. Just an emotional moment. Don't mind me."

A chuckle bubbled up her throat. "Yeah, I get it." The corners of her own eyes brimmed with tears.

"Ellie."

She twirled toward the familiar voice. Blake's brown hair was parted at the side and slicked flat against his skull. He brushed a bit of lint off his immaculate suit, tailored to fit his body to perfection.

"How've you been?" Ellie rubbed her elbow awkwardly. She and Blake had never had much in common. Small talk was the extent of their normal interactions.

"You know how the investment world is. Stocks are up, stocks are down."

Ellie pasted on a wide smile, inhaling enough air to dry out her front teeth. "Not really. The family business was always your and Dan's thing." In her periphery, Ellie spied her dad on his cell phone.

Blake's mouth twisted into a smirk. He straightened the Hermès tie sliding down his crisp poplin dress shirt. "Ah, yes. I forgot, rough-and-tumble activities are more your speed. How's your little cop thing going?"

Little cop thing?

"My very important and lifesaving job is going well, thank you." Ellie straightened her back, squaring her shoulders for good measure.

Blake had never taken her career choice seriously. To him, police officers were on the less lucrative side of the law. If it wouldn't make tons of money, Blake saw no reason to pursue it, no matter what it might be. He'd once told her that if she wanted to play cops and robbers so badly, she should've become a lawyer instead. At least that way she'd be making mint.

Her father popped up next to them and jiggled his phone in the air. "Wes sends his love from Europe."

"You finally managed to track him down?" Blake sighed

and pursed his lips. "Of course he finds out after all the drama's over and nothing's required of him. Typical Wesley."

That's harsh.

Ellie bit her lip. It wasn't like Wes planned for his trip to take place during a family emergency.

"You're not being fair." Their father placed a hand on Blake's shoulder. "He was a whole continent away when this happened. But he knows now, and Dan's better, and that's all that matters."

Blake's scowl softened but didn't disappear.

Ellie scanned the waiting room. For once, it was almost empty. She wasn't sure if that was good or bad. "Where's Mom?"

"In with Dan." Her father returned to his call.

"Wait, we can visit him? Why didn't you say so?" Ellie spun and hastened toward Dan's room.

When she sprang through the door, her mother beamed and held a finger to her lips, motioning for Ellie to be quiet. A doctor with a stethoscope stood over Dan, listening to his chest. Ellie tiptoed into a corner and waited.

"Everything sounds perfect, Dan." Dr. Bridget Undergrove's strawberry-blond hair was pulled back into a prim chignon. She picked up a clipboard and flipped through the attached pages before turning to Ellie's mother. Her mellow voice rolled around the room like honey off a flute spoon. "I think we're out of the woods, Mrs. Kline."

Ellie's heart swelled. *Dan's going to be okay.* More tears flooded her vision. She swiped them away with a grin.

While Dr. Undergrove and her mother discussed Dan's ongoing care for the immediate future, Ellie snuck over and kissed her brother's forehead. "How are you doing?"

Dan winced and lifted a hand to his side. The medicine and fluid IVs attached to his arm quivered. "I feel like garbage." A pale-gray tint still ran beneath his skin, but splotches of pink were returning to his cheeks. He inhaled and exhaled slowly, like the mere act of breathing exhausted him.

"Miss Kline?" After Dr. Undergrove caught Ellie's attention, she dropped a pen in the pocket of her white lab coat and pointed at the door. "May I have a word?"

That doesn't sound good.

Helen just shrugged as she resumed fussing over Dan.

Ellie frowned and trailed behind the doctor into the hall. A nurse passed by, pushing a patient in a wheelchair.

"Are you the one who advised us to check your brother for Vecuronium bromide?" Dr. Undergrove's rectangular eyeglass frames slid down her nose.

"Yes, that was me."

The doctor smiled wide, stretching the Cupid's bow of her upper lip flat. "Good call. You might have saved your brother's life. We gave him a neutralizer to counteract the Vecuronium bromide. We also flushed out his system and gave him a blood transfusion. It's speeding up his recovery."

"That's great. I'm glad I could help." Ellie's gaze drifted to the boxy window at the edge of the door to Dan's room. Her mother hovered over his bed, tucking a thick blanket in around his legs. Ellie couldn't tear herself away from the mesmerizing scene.

Dan survived. And I may have saved him.

"I believe we both know you did more than simply help." Dr. Undergrove placed a hand on Ellie's shoulder. "I just wanted to offer my appreciation for your assistance. Now go back in and enjoy spending time with your brother."

Once Ellie returned to the room, she hesitated. Dan was awake and coherent enough that she could ask him questions, but her mother would view the intrusion as unnecessary. The timing was far from ideal, but people were dying at an alarming rate in this case. She had no other choice. She needed to find out what Dan knew.

Clearing her throat, she stepped up beside his bed. "I'm happy you're okay, Dan, and I really hate that I have to bother you. But if I want to catch the guy who drugged you, I need to ask you a few questions."

Helen gaped. "Oh, no. No, no, no. This is not the time, Eleanor."

Ellie locked eyes with her mother. "We're out of time. Since Dan's ordeal, another person has died, and the killer is getting more violent. As long as he's still out there, Dan is still in danger too."

"I really don't think you should be bothering him so soon after he's woken up." The wrinkles on her mother's forehead deepened.

Dan's voice broke through their stare-down. "Mom, it's okay. I can help catch the guy who did this." He tilted his head toward Ellie. "What do you want to know?"

Ellie waited for her mother's nod of reluctant approval before responding. "Is there anything else you remember about the black-tie event? Maybe another argument, or a person getting emotional?"

"It's like I said…" When Dan's voice trailed off in a croak, Helen grabbed a paper cup from the table beside the hospital bed, urging him to take a sip. He sounded better when he continued. "Monique argued with her daughter and had a heated discussion with the server. Beyond that, the event was boring as hell."

Ellie rummaged in her bag and retrieved a stack of photos. "Do you think you can recall what the server looked like? Could you point him out from these photos?"

Dan took the stack and flipped through the pictures, pausing to study each one before moving on to the next with squinting eyes. "My memory's still a little fuzzy, but, out of all of these, this one sticks out. I'm pretty sure this was the guy."

He handed Ellie a photo. She sucked in a sharp breath so fast, the air tickled her throat and spurred a coughing fit. Her mother fetched another paper cup, filled it with water, and passed the drink to Ellie. She gulped the liquid down and gazed at the photo in her hand.

A man with large biceps and the tiniest sprigs of blond hair sprouting from his head smiled back at her. His hair was so light and short, he almost looked bald.

Gregory Chavin.

33

Clouds hung thick around the building as Ellie maneuvered her SUV into the precinct parking lot. After she pulled into a space and unbuckled her seat belt, an exaggerated sigh escaped her lips.

The second she opened the door, the humidity smacked her in the face. Reaching over the center console, she grabbed her bag from the passenger seat. Greg Chavin's photo, the one Dan identified as belonging to the mystery man at the mayor's black-tie event, peeked out from the top.

Could following up on the photo ID wait until Monday morning? Probably, but she'd risk letting the lead slip through her fingers. If Greg Chavin was the killer, he'd taken out three people already and attacked a fourth. Who knew what else the man was capable of?

And did it mean Jackie LaPierre was an accomplice? Or a potential victim too?

Last night was exactly what Ellie needed. Chomping on popcorn while she and Beth enjoyed an old sci-fi movie refreshed her. She desperately wished she had more of that bonding time. Lately, she'd been feeling like she was neglecting her foster daughter and under-delivering on her promises.

Instead of beating herself up, Ellie tried to focus on the positive. *Dan woke up. Not only that, he also identified a suspect for the case.* She raised her chin and glanced at the rearview mirror. *Get your shit together. There's no time for this pity party. You have a killer to catch, and you're doing the best you can.*

Walking across the parking lot, she pulled at the damp fabric of her blouse. The last time she checked the weather app on her phone, the temperature was in the low eighties. But by the time she'd marched into the precinct, her clothes stuck to her body like plastic wrap to static electricity.

When Ellie entered the bullpen, she arched an eyebrow at the sight of Lancaster hunched over his desk. "What are you doing?"

He sank farther into his chair, scrolling a finger over his phone. "I'm going over some paperwork, and we had a cheek swab appointment I wanted to be sure and supervise." He nodded toward the room in the back set up for the testing.

Donna Montague and Quint Bannister sat in plastic chairs. A uniform produced a swab from a packet. Quint's mouth was open so wide, he looked like a snake with its jaw unhinged, ready to devour a helpless animal. Donna hovered beside him, frowning as she watched the uniformed man swab her lover's cheek.

Ellie gasped, her eyes widening in disbelief. From her previous encounters with the duo, she'd expected them to blow off the appointment. Blinking, she dropped her bag in her desk chair and wandered over to Lancaster. "Wow. I thought they'd give us trouble."

"People haven't been kicking up much fuss about the cheek swabs. Although, we don't have complete compliance yet. While there are still many names on my list, we're getting there. Slowly but surely." He rested his elbows on his desk and stared at her, genuine concern radiating from his soft brown eyes. "How's your brother doing?"

Ellie grinned as a calming warmth settled into her chest. "Amazing. He woke up this morning." She still couldn't believe Dan was going to be okay. Or that she'd played a part in saving his life, thanks to the M.E.'s dedication to her job.

I need to send Dr. Faizal a gift basket or something. Maybe flowers or a cookie bouquet.

Lancaster's expression melted into one of confusion. "What are you doing here, then? Go to the hospital and be with your family. I've got this under control."

"I could ask you the same question. Quint Bannister's shady, but you don't have to be here supervising." Ellie took in the brown cargo shorts and teal polo shirt he wore in lieu of his usual suit and tie.

"It's fine." Lancaster slumped and shook his head. "Besides, right now, these cheek swabs are priority."

He grunted, his eyes flickering over to Quint and Donna as they exited the testing room. Donna raised her chin and ignored them on her way to the precinct lobby. Her three-inch heels *click-clicked*, and her beige chino pants swished as she strutted across the floor.

Quint followed dutifully behind her, wearing skintight jeans and a stupid smirk on his face. A bouncy whistle weaseled out from his lips when he passed them. Once he reached the door to the homicide department, he twisted around, puffed out his chest, and snapped his fingers in triumph. "Later, gators."

Ellie rolled her eyes and parked her behind on the edge of Lancaster's desk. "So where are we with the rest of the list? Specifically, White Gloves Catering. Have all the employees come in for their cheek swabs?"

If my hunch about Chavin is right, he'll be avoiding the precinct like it's the plague.

And she'd have some explaining to do. Stoddard wouldn't be pleased upon discovering that she'd withheld information from Lancaster. Her boss made it clear they were supposed to work together on this case.

Guilt tugged at Ellie, weaving its way upward and taking root in the back of her mind. A dull ache throbbed at the base of her neck. At some point—and soon—she'd have to come clean to Lancaster and her boss about the evidence she neglected to share. She crossed her arms, dreading the thought of that conversation.

Lancaster leaned back in his chair and swiveled from side to side. "The manager insisted his staff cooperate. We're one hundred percent done with that group. Everyone complied."

Her eyebrows shot up. *Everyone? Including Greg Chavin?* "You're sure all the employees showed up and provided samples? Every single one?"

Maybe Dan was mistaken. He was drunk at the event, and he's on pain meds now. It's possible he identified the wrong man.

Lancaster picked up a printout and ran his finger down the list of names. "Yeah, I was a little shocked, too, considering folks with pasts like the employees of White Gloves Catering usually prefer to avoid…wait a minute." An exasperated groan escaped his throat.

"What?" Ellie scooted off the desk and leaned over his shoulder. Black letters and checkmarks dotted the white paper.

"I was mistaken. We don't have one-hundred-percent compliance with White Gloves Catering. One guy didn't show up for his scheduled appointment yesterday. Damn." He slammed the paper on the top of his desk before Ellie could fully examine the list.

"Who?" She swallowed, her saliva scratching down her dry throat like sand. A fire churned in her gut. She already knew the answer. Lancaster confirming the suspicion was a simple formality.

Because Dan wasn't wrong.

"Gregory Chavin. He's the only one we're missing."

She closed her eyes. *There's only one reason Chavin would avoid having his DNA taken. He's got to be the father of Monique's unborn baby.*

A motive for Monique's murder, as well as Bernard's death and her brother's poisoning. Bernard used his position as Coastline Inn security to tamper with the cameras so Chavin could take care of Monique. He knew too much. And her brother saw Chavin arguing with Monique. Which meant he also knew too much.

That left Kira. Why did Chavin consider her a threat? Ellie frowned. There wasn't much to establish a connection between the two. Just the LaPierre Foundation.

He was a former LaPierre recipient. In their meeting the other day, Kira mentioned that she, as the foundation's director, handled everything for the charity. And her murder was the most vicious. Something she did in that role made Chavin hate her. Was it possible he was involved in the court cases Clay mentioned, the ones brought against LaPierre?

The possibility seemed odd. If her assumptions were correct, Chavin was romantically linked to both Monique and Jackie LaPierre. Why would he get involved with both of them if he'd tried to sue the family?

If he was part of the failed court cases, it's possible he never lost his grudge with the LaPierre Foundation.

"Did you hear me? This guy Chavin skipped out on—"

Ellie raised a finger, and Lancaster stopped talking.

The hum of an old-school clock on the wall caught Ellie's ear.

Imagine Chavin hated the LaPierre Foundation, but his

attempts to take the nonprofit down flopped. So he went after the family behind the foundation instead.

Only a cold, calculating person would concoct such a long-term revenge plot.

Could Greg Chavin be a man with such Machiavellian aspirations?

Opening her eyes, she scurried to her desk and fetched her bag from the chair. She motioned for Lancaster to follow her. "Buckle up. You and I are rolling. I'm driving."

He stood and slipped his phone into his pocket. "Going where, exactly?"

Ellie yelled over her shoulder while she raced to the department exit. "I was just at the hospital, showing my brother photos of the catering staff. He identified Gregory Chavin as the person he saw arguing with Monique the night of the party. We need to find Chavin ASAP."

34

The thick-ass walls in Jackie's mansion closed in on me. I paced the room in frantic strides, still unsure how to wiggle my way out of this one. In the background, the TV blared.

"Daniel Kline Jr., Charleston resident and member of the affluent Kline family, has woken from his coma and is expected to make a full recovery. According to our sources, Kline fell ill after ingesting the drug Vecuronium bromide, normally used as anesthesia in surgeries. How he ingested the drug is still in question, but police ask that any residents with any infor—"

Grabbing the remote, I clicked off the television.

Fuck!

My phone buzzed again. Yanking the device from my back pocket, I stared at the screen. A dozen missed calls and even more ignored texts from my boss.

Cheek swab. Remember appointment today.
Cops called. U missed appt. Reschedule.
Pick up the phone. Cops calling to reschedule appt.
R u putting off the cheek swab?

This was getting out of control. *I* was getting out of control. Once people knew I was the father of Monique's baby, they'd figure out I killed her. Of course I was avoiding that cheek swab.

Icy chills swept down my spine. My heart thudded against my rib cage. *This is bad.* The muscles in my legs and arms stiffened, and I stopped pacing.

Why the hell were the cops so interested now? When I was growing up, plenty of my friends had suffered far worse fates than Dan Kline Jr. They disappeared or died. The cops gave zero shits, not interested enough to even find out why or how.

No, those bastards didn't care unless the victim belonged to the wealthy elite. Low-rent gutter kids like me and the others? We were the dog shit the rich folk kicked off their heels.

Justice was for the haves, not the have-nots. I learned that lesson young, when Kira arranged my first meeting with some affluent guy in his sixties. The bitch didn't care what he did to me, or forced me to do, as long as she got her cut of the pay.

I tried to fight back. So did some of the other kids. We found a lawyer who took us on pro bono and got a case going against LaPierre.

But after one kid disappeared, the lawyer dropped us before our case made it to court. Said we didn't have a viable cause or enough supporting evidence. *We* were the proof. Our bruises and scars and traumas. But we were poor nobodies.

We just got tossed back into the system and shuffled around again, discarded like yesterday's trash. After being reprimanded by Kira and her goons, of course.

The damn heels of my shoes squeaked as I stormed into the kitchen. They were a pair of Louboutins Jackie bought for me right after we first started dating, so I'd fit in more. Or embarrass her less. I could never be sure. Three hundred dollars of fancy leather, and I still couldn't catch a break. Even the expensive things I owned didn't respect me.

My eyes landed on a loaf of Italian bread resting on a cutting board at the end of the counter. Beside the chopping block, sunlight bounced off a large serrated knife. The sharp edges glistened like polished teeth.

I jerked open the refrigerator, the condiments shaking and rattling as the door slammed against the cabinet. Reaching inside, I grabbed a plastic bin of thick-cut shaved turkey, a jar of mayo, and a pack of Swiss. A stinky aroma floated through the air when I ripped open the package of cheese.

Peeling a slice of Swiss and turkey, I rolled them together and shoved the whole thing into my dry mouth. *How should I handle this?* I'd never come this close to getting caught. At least, not without a plan on how to get away.

"Babe?"

I dragged my gaze to the kitchen doorway.

Jackie stood there, wearing yet another pair of leggings and an oversize shirt. Her dark curls hung limp around her face. At one point, seducing her was a necessity. Now I wanted to punch her mopey face every time it popped out in front of me.

I've come this far, though. Gotta keep playing the game.

I waved my hand over the food. "You want a sandwich? I'm buying."

She shook her head. "No. Hey, I just got a strange call from Ellie, my friend in the police department. She wanted to know if I'd seen you today. Why would she call and ask me that?"

Because the cops are on to me. They know I murdered your mom, and Bernard, and Kira. Oh, and I tried and failed to take out the cop's brother.

I shrugged, struggling to swallow the bite of cheese and

turkey lodged in my throat. "Dunno. Maybe she has more questions about the party. You look tired, Jacks. Sure I can't make you some food? You got to keep your strength up."

"No, I'm..." Jackie shook her head again and huffed. The tip of her pink tongue twisted between her teeth. "Don't change the subject. She sounded really freaked out."

"Hell if I know what she wants." I twirled the lid off the mayo jar. Slowly. My head cocked to the side. *Play it casual.* The silverware in the drawer clanked when I pulled a butter knife from the tray. "So what did you tell her?"

Jackie shuffled into the kitchen with her mouth pinched into an unflattering pout. "I said of course I've seen you. You live here. I see you every day." She leaned her fat ass against the counter and crossed her arms. Her judgy glare boiled my blood.

"Her brother's out of his coma. Maybe that's why she sounded weird. Lot of stuff going on." I kept my voice even and focused on building my sandwich, avoiding her eyes. "Did you tell her I was here?"

She scoffed, a sound I'd grown to hate in our time together. "Uh, yes. Babe, what's this about? Are you in trouble again?"

Fuck yes. And trapped.

My mind raced, trying to calculate how long I had until the cops showed up. The call to Jackie confirmed they were on to me. I could run, but where the hell would I go?

For months, I'd played the role of the good boyfriend to squeeze as much as I could from those bitches. When Kira dummied my records at the foundation to label me as a failed recipient, Monique took a special interest. I was a reject who couldn't be helped, but she wanted to try.

Monique couldn't stand leaving any of LaPierre's kids behind. Yet she never looked close enough at her precious foundation to realize the horrific mistreatment some of us suffered.

When she got me out of juvie and found me a job, I saw my chance for revenge.

Jackie. The resentful and rebellious little rich girl.

I waited until her old man died to make my move. He'd never have approved of me. One of LaPierre's pity cases? Not for his spoiled princess. As soon as he kicked the bucket, I wormed my way into Jackie's heart. Her pants too.

All those years being groomed by Kira's clients made trapping Jackie in my web a breeze.

Monique was harder. Even after Hal died, she remained devoted to her husband. Once a few months passed, though, even *she* couldn't say no to her daughter's kindhearted boyfriend and a bottle of wine.

All the while, I raked in the gifts and luxuries. Fancy dinners and lavish trips. The plan was to live the good life for as long as I could. Maybe even marry Jackie one day, sans a prenup. After a year or two, I could dump her ass and enjoy my divorce settlement while reveling in the fact that I'd broken both Jackie's and Monique's hearts.

But fucking Monique had to get pregnant. In her fifties. And then she wanted to ruin my entire plan.

Now Jackie was destroying everything. With her stupid cop friend and her mopey face crying on my shoulder all the time. This plan stopped being fun a long time ago.

My chest heaved. The blood pounding in my ears intensified the rage building inside me.

I need this to end.

My fingers inched closer to the knife by the bread loaf and wrapped around the wooden handle.

35

The siren on the roof of Ellie's SUV wailed as the vehicle's tires slid on the road like paper pinwheels in a tornado.

She clocked their location. About halfway to Jackie's. Another car swerved out of the lane to let her pass. She pressed her foot harder on the gas pedal.

Lancaster lurched forward and slapped his hand against the dash. "You've got to slow down, or we're going to crash into something."

Keep nagging, and the only cold crash here will be my patience hitting rock bottom.

Ignoring him, Ellie hooked a hard right.

Clay's voice vibrated through the speakers. "We've been able to link Gregory Chavin to a few of the abuse cases against the LaPierre Foundation. The last one was nasty. Lots of extremely dark accusations."

"When was this?"

Bile rose in the back of Ellie's throat. She didn't want to imagine what those dark accusations comprised.

Those poor kids.

The *click* of a mouse punctuated Clay's words as he spoke.

"Chavin was sixteen. We don't know why, but he withdrew his claim."

Sixteen?

Ellie leaned in toward the speaker. "I don't understand. He said Monique found him when he was eighteen after a six-month stint in juvie."

"And that's true. Kind of. Monique took him under her wing, probably because he was one of their few failed cases, but Chavin originally entered LaPierre's program when he was twelve."

Ellie's jaw dropped. *Twelve?* That was only a few years older than Bethany. She imagined Beth dancing in the living room and rolling in the grass with the dogs. Kids were supposed to have fun and be free. What kind of monster would rob them of that, and for such insidious purposes?

"What were his claims? For the court cases?" She lifted her foot off the gas pedal and maneuvered her way through traffic at a red light, honking at cars that didn't stop or move out of her way. Once she was safe on the other side, she slammed her foot back onto the pedal.

"For the love of…" Lancaster grunted and gripped the grab handle above the door as the shuddering SUV barreled down the road.

Clay sucked in a sharp breath. "Chavin says he was groomed from the moment LaPierre took him in and used by LaPierre's elite contacts for their own purposes. I won't go into detail, but he talks about performing some pretty nonconsensual acts. If rage is a motivator in your case, trust me, Greg Chavin probably has it in spades."

Ellie punched her sternum, trying to push the bile back down. "Anything else on Greg?"

"No." Clay's voice lowered. "Ellie, be careful. This guy has possibly killed three people already. He's dangerous. You guys need to call for backup."

"I acknowledge your request. Thanks, Clay." Ellie rolled her eyes and disconnected the call before he could protest. She'd assess the situation first.

The day she'd met him, Chavin had mentioned foster homes, but he hadn't said anything about being a LaPierre recipient from the age of twelve. In fact, he gave Ellie the impression he didn't enter LaPierre's system until he was older.

I wonder if Jackie knows about Chavin's history with LaPierre and the accusations? Or, for that matter, if Monique knew?

The foundation was named after the family, but from what she'd gathered over the years from her mom and her own interactions, the LaPierres maintained a hands-off approach regarding the day-to-day business of running the charity. They were the faces in front of—and money behind—the nonprofit. They left everything else to people like Kira Long.

Ellie still couldn't wrap her brain around Chavin's endgame. More than a decade had passed since he accused the LaPierre Foundation of abuse, and now he was playing house with Jackie LaPierre? From what Clay said, the guy should despise the family, yet he'd wedged himself into their lives instead. Why?

"I still don't understand." Lancaster cursed under his breath as Ellie drifted around a corner. "If Chavin's the killer, and if he has such a huge grudge against the LaPierre Foundation, why the hell is he involved with Jackie LaPierre? Why is he working a job the foundation provided to him? You think this is some kind of long con to get revenge?"

Ellie side-eyed him. *Did he just read my mind?*

"You and I are on the same page." Her fingers tightened around the steering wheel. "I don't know what game he's playing. I only know the facts. Chavin's reluctant to get his cheek swabbed. Why? Because he's the father of Monique's child. Dan identified Greg Chavin as the server Monique argued with the night she died."

She swerved around another corner onto an older road. Fewer and fewer houses popped up, with large swaths of trees and fields filling the gap between them. Gravel crunched and whirled beneath the tires. Random rocks shot up into the air, clanging against the SUV's exterior.

Lancaster frowned. "To be fair, your brother had just woken up from a coma and was still flying high on hospital-grade drugs. He could've made a mistake." He squeezed his eyes shut, refusing to observe their ascent as they soared over a small hill in the road.

The LaPierre mansion was a mere mile away.

"True. But I trust him. There's also the fact that Chavin works in pharmaceuticals." She'd learned Chavin's profession during her first visit to the LaPierre mansion. "Both Bernard Cookson and my brother were poisoned by the same paralytic drug used in anesthesia."

Lancaster snapped his head toward her. "Wait, what? What drug? How do you know that?"

Ellie swallowed hard. "Does it matter right now?" She would explain later. "Just listen. That drug was something Chavin most likely had access to, as well as a basic knowledge of how to use it. What better way to take care of the loose ends he'd left lying around?"

Lancaster groaned as Ellie whipped down the final side road toward the LaPierre mansion. They passed a pond with a weeping willow similar to the ones lining the driveway to the home. Branches drooped over the water, leaves still in the dead air.

Ellie eased her foot off the accelerator. The spires at the top of the wrought iron gate to the mansion appeared.

Jackie had claimed Chavin was with her when Ellie called. *Has she mentioned our conversation to him yet?* Ellie bit her lip, wishing her friend hadn't hung up before she could tell her to hunker down, stay safe, and wait for her arrival.

Her thoughts scrambled to assess her friend's peril. Greg Chavin would feel cornered. Trapped.

A car up ahead forced them to slow down considerably. Ellie slammed her palm against the center of the steering wheel. A long, loud *beep* bellowed while she careened past the vehicle in front. In the passenger seat, Lancaster covered his ears with a clenched hand.

Even if Chavin truly loved Jackie and their entire relationship *wasn't* a twisted revenge plot, he could still lash out at her. Blame her. Hurt her. The ways in which he could channel his anger toward Jackie were endless.

Worst-case scenarios raced through her mind. Shallow breaths pierced her lungs in staccato beats. When her eyes darted to the dashboard's digital clock, her heart sank. How much time had passed since she hung up the phone with Jackie? Tears stung her eyes. She wasn't sure.

What if we're too late?

Ellie only knew one thing for certain.

Jackie was in danger, and each wasted second dropped another nail into her coffin.

36

For every step Greg took forward, Jackie stole two backward, until her back was flat against the kitchen wall. Sweat glazed her skin. She wiped her clammy hands on her leggings.

What the hell is going on? One minute, he's making a sandwich. The next, he's got a knife and I'm trying to talk him down.

She'd almost missed the subtle shift, from familiar to homicidal, in his face. Like in the movies, when the special effects dude overlaid a possessed character's face with the ghost's image. Her heart thundered against her chest at the sight of the shadows clouding his expression. She gulped and kept her eyes trained on the serrated blade in his hand.

He isn't right. Why is he all wrong?

Below his frosty blue eyes, Greg's cheeks flushed red hot. A vein beneath the tattoo on his bicep pulsed as he stalked toward her, his gaze dark and menacing. "How much did she tell you about what happened to Monique? Your little friend, the detective? And what have you told her?"

Jackie gaped, not knowing what to do. Her first instinct

was to run. *But...this is Greg. The guy who cared for me after Mom died. The one person I trust most in the world and who truly understands me.*

"Did you forget how to fucking talk? Answer me." Greg's eyes narrowed, and the hand holding the knife twitched. He smirked, *tsk-tsk*ing at her. "I get it. You think you can stall me until she shows up, huh? Until she fastens the cuffs around my wrists? That the plan you two cooked up on the phone?"

Realization pummeled Jackie like a bag of bricks. Her stomach plummeted.

It's him.

That was the only reason she could fathom that he'd be standing in her kitchen, brandishing a knife, and quizzing her on Ellie's progress on her mother's murder case.

No. That was impossible. Right?

Ask him. He'll say no and have some explanation for whatever's going on.

"Greg, did you kill my mom?" The words scraped up her throat.

A long stretch of silence swallowed her.

She twisted a loose string on the hem of her shirt around her finger. Holding her breath. Waiting.

Why isn't he saying anything?

His lips curved into a sneer. "Seriously? What gave me away, Jacks? The knife or the threats?"

The laugh shocked and sickened her. Wave after wave of acid roared in her stomach. Her head felt like a balloon on a delicate string, moments from drifting away into a sky of nothingness.

Greg's the killer. The asshole who murdered my mom. Jackie ground her teeth, letting the hatred drench her. Heat raged across her skin. *He's a liar and a murderer. And he robbed me of the only family I had left.*

"You bastard. I fucking loved you." She dodged to the side, attempting to evade Greg and his knife.

"If you love me so much, why do you keep running away? Huh?" He grasped her arm, digging his fingernails into her wrist. As Greg shoved her back, he blocked her escape route.

She recoiled, disgusted by the way his touch still electrified her. "Get away from me. Mom was on your fucking side. Why did you kill her?" Tears slid down her blazing cheeks. Gulping back a sob, she swiped the tears with her hand, smearing them across her face.

"My side? She was on my side?" He took another step toward her and waved the blade wildly, the knife slicing through empty space. "When did I ever have anyone on my side? My parents died. The foster home didn't give a shit where I ended up as long as I was far away from them. And your family? Your LaPierre Foundation? You guys were the worst."

The worst?

White-hot anger burned in Jackie's chest, like a light bulb on the verge of shorting out. Her parents never hurt anyone. They helped people. They cared. His accusation stung the pride she carried for her mother and father and all the good work they'd done in their lives.

"Why? We saved you, you jerk." Jackie's heart pounded, the pulse radiating from the top of her head to the tip of her toes. Her stomach coiled into knots.

Oxygen...where did all the oxygen go? I can't breathe.

"That's what you think, huh? They saved me? Bullshit. The minute I got tied up with the LaPierre Foundation, my life became a thousand times more horrific. Don't you know what was going on, Jackie? They groomed me. Sent me to rich people's bedrooms in exchange for money. I had to do whatever they wanted. Whatever depraved and disgusting act they paid for. And not just me. Lots of the kids. A few even vanished. Never came back from their appointments. No one cared. LaPierre just sent out another kid."

A fresh round of sobs consumed Jackie, and her chest heaved in staggered bursts. "You're lying. That's trafficking. My parents would never—"

"Are you sure? Okay, I'll fucking give them the benefit of the doubt. They didn't know. The whole setup was Kira Long's doing. But you know what? In my mind, that makes your parents even worse. Because they *should've* known. It was their job to know. They failed me. They failed all of us."

"All of us? I've known you since Mom got you out of juvie. What the hell are you talking about?" Jackie spun toward the counter. Her hands landed on a large wooden bowl holding a few apples. Gripping the rim, she thrust the dish at his head.

Two of the apples made contact, but the bowl missed and clattered to the floor, spiraling to a stop in front of Greg. He glared and kicked, sending the dish sailing against the wall so hard it splintered and cracked. His eyes bored into Jackie's.

"Monique never told you? I'd been in the LaPierre foundation's program for years by that time. Your mom didn't recognize me at first. She and your dad spent all their time fundraising and hobnobbing with other rich people. No, your mom found me because my file had been closed as a failed case. A red mark on the ledger."

Jackie pressed her hands to her temples. "I don't understand."

"I didn't want her pity, but I let her take pity on me. I wanted to get even, and she viewed me as some lame bird with a broken fucking wing she could fix. The best attack is unexpected. She never saw me coming."

Her chest tightened. She pressed her trembling hand against her heart. "You killed my mom...because she didn't know something?" Sadness spilled into her soul. The anger fueling her faltered.

How could Mom have died for such a stupid reason?

Greg knocked a chair aside, causing Jackie to yelp. "You and your kind think you're so great because you have money. Wealth solves everything, doesn't it? You rich snobs don't give a shit about the normal people."

Jackie wrapped her arms around her torso. "But I do care." Didn't she? Her whole life was spent rebelling against the role of a spoiled princess. She volunteered at charities, donated her old clothes, and gave decent amounts of money to churches and soup kitchens.

Isn't that enough?

"Oh, really? This house has ten bedrooms. Do you know how many families could get off the streets? People who sit in the rain and the cold and the heat and go hungry and thirsty and sick because they don't have money? Your car, the BMW out there? Sell that, and they'd be able to eat for a year too. But no. It's your house, your car, your money. And people like you don't like to share."

Jackie's nostrils flared, and the fire in her chest returned, burning so bright she thought she'd melt. "I *do* care, you asshole. I've spent most of my life volunteering and rejecting what I never felt like I'd earned because I wasn't born into this family. And I fucking loved you with all of my heart."

Her eyes darted to the right. An opening appeared near the wall and the table, separating her from Greg. She licked her lips and weighed her chances.

Run.

She made a mad dash for it. He lunged at her with the knife, narrowly missing as she shimmied through the space and scurried through the kitchen door. Heavy footfalls chased her, growing closer and closer. She sprinted toward the front door and grasped the handle, praying she'd escape in time. As she flung the large barrier open, a bright, blinding light shot into the dark, gloomy foyer.

Jackie covered her eyes with her forearm and rushed out onto the porch. Just before she reached the steps, a muscular arm hooked her waist and threw her to the ground.

No!

"Nice try. It's time to pay your dues, little rich girl." Greg's beefy fingers encircled her ankles, and he dragged her back toward the house.

She clawed at the edge of the porch, fingernails breaking as she dug into the concrete. Jackie tried to flip around and kick him, but Greg stomped against her lower back. Hard enough to knock the wind out of her.

As he pulled her farther into the house, she released a piercing scream. When the door shut, the light vanished, eaten once again by the foyer's shadows.

Behind her, Greg laughed, yanking her hair until she rose and stood facing him. The murderous glint in his eyes wilted her courage. He traced the knife along the edge of her chin.

Jackie caught their reflection in a gilded mirror on the other side of the room. The image of Greg towering over her helpless body terrified her.

She'd almost depleted her energy to fight back. Emotionally, she was drained.

But I'm not going down without a fight.

Mustering all her strength, she jammed her elbow deep into his rib cage. The *oof* that broke from his lips as his grasp on her loosened and he doubled over reinvigorated Jackie. She bolted for the front door, racing until her hand grazed the knob.

Pain exploded in her head, and as the world faded to a wall of gray dots, Jackie struggled to stay upright in the suddenly spinning room. *What...?*

Her body hit the floor with a *thud*. She blinked several

times, trying to focus as something warm and sticky dripped around her ear.

A thick vase rolled into her view. Drops of water and loose rose petals from a sympathy arrangement for her mother's death still clung to it. She blinked again. A familiar pair of Louboutins stepped around the vase.

Greg crouched over her, a sneer slithering across his face as he ran the blade down her neck, stopping at her clavicle. He leaned down and whispered, his voice a guttural growl.

"Poor little rich girl. Nobody can hear you. Not all the way out here in your castle made of blood money."

37

As Ellie pulled up to the LaPierre mansion, she spotted an old, beat-up green Volvo coated in dirt with a crushed-in driver's side door. Long, spidery cracks ran along the back window, and one of the taillights was smashed. On the other side of the driveway, a shiny BMW and new-model Lexus jeered at the Volvo.

The car stuck out like a chicken in a dog race. Or an abandoned house on the side of the road, akin to one of those splintering wood structures built at the turn of the century and left to suffer the ravages of nature. As Ellie skidded to a halt beside the out-of-place vehicle, her gut clenched.

They'd lost precious seconds arguing with the guard controlling the estate's wrought iron gate. By the time he relented and pressed the button to let them through, fear clamped stiff fingers around Ellie's heart.

Please tell me we're not too late.

She killed the engine and glanced at Lancaster. "Go around to the back. Find a way in. And we want to subdue him, not harm him, if possible. I still have a lot of questions Chavin needs to answer."

Ellie scurried out of the SUV and gripped her weapon, holding it at the ready. Save for a bird's song chiming through the treetops, the mansion and grounds were quiet.

Lancaster eased the passenger door shut and scanned the house. After unholstering his weapon, he shuffled toward the side of the mansion, keeping his head low.

Ellie climbed the steps two at a time and was banging her fist against the door a few seconds later. "Charleston Police, open up." The force of her knocks echoed in her ears.

She held her breath. There was a housekeeper. Did Jackie send her away? Or did Chavin have both the housekeeper and Jackie in there?

A breeze whipped through the air and rustled the leaves in the trees, and a couple more birds chittered on branches. Behind the door, the house remained silent.

Sweat dampened Ellie's upper lip. She swiped her hand across her mouth before hammering her fist against the door a second time. "Charleston PD. Open up!"

She pressed her ear to the wood. *Nothing. No, wait. What's that shuffling sound?* Ellie twisted the knob.

Of course it's locked. She exhaled harshly. Her eyes drifted to the cars in the driveway. *She should be here. Jackie, where are you?*

A bloodcurdling scream rose from the other side of the door. Another, softer cry followed.

"Charleston Police, entering the premises!"

Ellie hurled her body toward the shriek. The dense wood refused to give when she hammered her shoulder against the barrier. Undeterred, she stood back and kicked out, ramming her foot near the lock. On the sixth try, the wood buckled and knocked open, and she stumbled into the foyer.

Gripping the weapon with both hands, she aimed her

pistol in front of her. "Charleston Police, Detective Kline! Come out where I can see you."

The daylight from the open door broke through the shadows blanketing the entryway. She poked her head into a room on the right. While the windows' thick curtains were drawn, light filtered through the edges of the fabric. Enough for her to tell that the room was empty.

Her next stop was the room on the left, where she'd interviewed Jackie days before. Those curtains were shut so tight that Ellie could barely make out anything in the darkness. She pressed her back against the wall. Her fingers danced around her belt, stopping on her small flashlight.

Once Ellie clicked the switch, she peeked around the doorway. The light glided over furniture and books and cabinets. Otherwise, the room was empty.

"Help!" Jackie's voice pierced the foyer from a room farther back to the left. Terror poured from her plea. "He's got a knife. He's going to—"

A screech, raw and guttural like an injured animal, cut through the house. Ellie raced down the hallway, her heartrate skyrocketing as a series of crashes drowned Jackie's cries. She wheeled around a corner and skidded to a halt.

In the kitchen, Chavin pressed a serrated blade close to Jackie's neck, the veins in his bulky forearms bulging against the dark curls falling onto her shoulders. His other arm grappled her arms and torso. Crimson flushed his cheeks, and his nostrils flared wide.

Jackie's body shook against him as the blade flitted closer to her skin. Wet, matted hair stuck to the side of her face. Wiggling against his grasp, she struggled to break free from his hold. He shoved the tip of the blade into the flesh beneath her chin, drawing a sliver of blood. She stopped moving, her eyes bulging at Ellie.

"Put down the knife." Ellie inched her way into the kitchen.

"No! Are you fucking kidding?" Spittle flew from Chavin's lips when he screamed. "They got what they deserved. All of them. No one was ever going to find out the truth. I had to take the law into my own hands." As he gripped the knife, his knuckles turned white.

Ellie didn't have a plan. Sweat beaded on her forehead. A wrong move or word on her part could cost Jackie her life.

So keep him talking while you think of one. She stiffened her elbows. *And keep the gun on him.*

"But now we know. I know what happened. You were just a kid, and they groomed you." Ellie stepped toward Chavin, her eyes fixed on his. "They forced you into acts you didn't want. But Monique wasn't part of that, was she? She actually thought she was helping you."

His mouth trembled. "I don't want to talk about her."

But I need you to keep talking until Lancaster shows up or I get an opportunity to take you down.

Ellie cleared her throat, making sure her tone remained soft. Relatable. "Because she tried to save you? Or because she was pregnant with your child?"

From the corner of her eye, Ellie glimpsed Jackie's mouth dropping open. Glassy tears rained down her cheeks.

I'm sorry you had to find out this way.

Chavin sneered. "Yeah. After her husband died, she was a wreck. I played the part she needed. I was there for her. When she told me she was pregnant, I didn't believe her. I mean, she was in her fifties. But when she told me she was going to leave me, I lost it."

With small, slow steps, Ellie slid her feet along the marble. Closer to Chavin and his knife. "I understand."

"After everything she'd done for me, she was going to kick me to the curb. Like, she got me back on my feet just so she could throw me back down again. I'd started to like her too. Or at least, hate her less. Then she went and ruined it all. She was going to tell Jackie everything, and then where would that leave me?" He shook his arm, jostling a whimpering Jackie. "The bitch wanted to destroy my life. Just like the others."

"You were a victim." Ellie glanced at Jackie, who hung limp in Chavin's hold. "A victim of it all. We can help you, Greg. Really help you. If you let us."

He cocked his head, an eyebrow raised in disbelief. "Really? Even after what I did to Danny boy? You'd still stick your neck out for me?"

No.

Ellie bit the word back. Every cell in her body wanted him to pay for hurting her family. Her fists ached to bang against his bones and let the worry and stress of the last week wash away with each punch. *But that isn't justice.* Instead, she raised her chin and leveled her gaze.

"Vengeance only gets a person so far, Greg. Eventually, you have to let law and order take control."

His face contorted into a cruel smile as he laughed. "Poor people like me…the have-nots…don't get law and order. Haven't you been paying attention? The rich make the laws. They decide what's order and what's chaos. They do everything they can to stomp us down into the dirt. Not everyone's lucky enough to be born on the right side of the railroad tracks like you and her."

Ellie dropped her gaze to his arm, where Jackie's body swayed, her head low and her face painted with tears. No person chose what side of the tracks they were born on or what privileges they received. Wealth was the luck of the draw.

Some people had no money, but all the love in the world. Other people had all the money, but no love. The best anyone could do was work with whatever they had, love or wealth or both, to make a positive difference in the world.

Keep him talking, dammit.

"You're right. Jackie and I were lucky. I'm sorry you weren't. But you've got my attention now. I can help you." Ellie maintained eye contact as she continued to edge closer to him, centimeter by centimeter.

He scoffed. "You guys never help. I've gone to the police. So have some of the other victims of the trafficking ring. Some have even gotten as high as the FBI. Nothing changes. All our allegations just get swept under the rug by lawyers."

"And that wasn't right." Ellie shifted her gaze to the sides of the room. *Where the hell is Lancaster?* She'd sent him around back expecting him to find a way in to back her up.

Chavin's jaw hardened. "We're poor. We don't have the power they do. We don't have everyone in our back pocket, ready to clean up our messes. I thought if I killed Monique and Kira, the police would pay more attention to our claims and reveal the truth, but that's never going to happen, is it?"

"You're wrong. We're investigating Delecroix Logistics, and we've got a trail on them, but we need your assistance to nail these monsters to the wall." Ellie crept forward. "Put the knife down and help us, Greg."

"That's the truth?" The knife in his hand wavered as he lifted his chin in skepticism. "You're willing to take these people down?"

Ellie nodded and lowered her pistol a half inch. "Yes. Put the knife down. Let Jackie go. Then this can end peacefully, and we can start talking about a game plan to get you the justice you deserve." She licked her lips. "You can testify against them, maybe even get witness protection."

Though his eyes dropped to the frightened woman in his arms, the knife didn't budge from Jackie's neck.

I'm losing him. Get him ranting. Maybe he'll let his guard down and I'll get an opening to rescue Jackie. What does he hate?

The memory of Kira's bloodied body seared into Ellie's mind. Tilting her head to the side, she lowered her chin. "And you can also tell me about Kira. We can tell everyone who she really was. I'll help you."

"Kira?" Chavin's focus shot back to Ellie. "That bitch was the one who orchestrated most of it. She took the payments and farmed us out. Looked the other way. We were just kids, and she passed us around from abusive home to abusive home. The meet and greets we had to take part in? All Kira's handiwork."

The payments from Delecroix. The fancy lifestyle. The hatred in Kira's murder. All of it makes sense now.

"I can imagine how traumatic that was, for all of you. How difficult it was watching her flash all the money she made off your backs. Put the knife down, Greg. So you can tell me everything." Ellie's pulse quickened, and a trickle of sweat slid down her neck.

Chavin used Jackie as a shield to cover much of his body, and the way she kept moving in his grasp prevented Ellie from getting a clear shot if the need arose. Ellie scanned her periphery for any movement or sign of Lancaster. Still nowhere in sight. Her blood pounded in her veins.

I have to keep stalling him.

"Come on, Greg. We can sit down and hash this all out. Just us. After you let Jackie go, you can tell me what pushed you over the edge. Why you had to take care of Monique and Kira." Ellie swallowed hard as a stony-faced Chavin studied her.

"I told you. I thought Monique's death would make people look closer. When they didn't, I decided Kira was next in line." His eyes blazed, and his mouth twisted into a crooked snarl. He licked his lips. "Plus, I really, *really* hated that bitch. Killing her was much more fun than the others."

Ellie steadied her aim on Chavin. His breathing intensified as he spoke, causing his chest to heave. The thumb gripping the knife quivered.

One move, and he could slice right into Jackie's throat.

She stepped forward, slow and steady. "Greg, if we work together, we can end this for—"

A brick crashed through the window of a side door. Shattering glass exploded into the room. Ellie grimaced but maintained her position.

Chavin whirled toward the disruption, the knife drawing away from Jackie. "The hell?"

Now's my chance.

Ellie jumped into action, using the distraction to try and smack the weapon from his fingers.

Before she could make contact, he spun and pushed the blade closer to Jackie's neck. He wobbled between Ellie and the source of the noise. "What the fuck is happening? How did you do that?"

Lancaster materialized amid the shards of what was once a deck door, his gun aimed right at Chavin. "Charleston PD, get your hands up!"

Chavin shifted, but he kept a firm hold on Jackie as she tried to slither from his grasp. Tensing, he pointed the knife at Lancaster. "Who the hell are you?"

"I said get your hands up. Let the lady go and get those damn hands up, or I'll shoot." Lancaster's brown eyes darkened.

Ellie stared at Jackie. The poor woman was the very definition of terrified. *How did I lose control of this situation so quickly?* Her own gaze shifted to the other detective. "Lancaster, wait."

Howling, Chavin raised the knife, the blade aimed at Jackie's chest. He brought his arm down, hard and fast.

Before the knife could reach Jackie's body, two shots from Lancaster's gun rang out. Jackie screamed when the bullets whizzed past her and burrowed into Chavin's shoulder. His body dropped to the ground, his heavy arm dragging Jackie to the floor with him. She scrambled onto her knees and crawled behind the kitchen island.

Ellie ducked as Lancaster raised his gun again and pointed the barrel at Chavin. "Lancaster, don't! He's down. He's down."

She stared, horrified, first at her partner and then at Chavin. A splotchy circle of blood seeped into the fibers of Chavin's shirt, growing larger and larger.

A *bang* thundered across the kitchen when Lancaster fired his gun again.

Ellie lunged forward and grappled at the hulking man. His weapon remained in front of him, ready to shoot a fourth time. His ruthless glare rattled Ellie to her core.

That look...why does it scare me?

She bashed a fist against his arm and shoved the gun toward the floor. "Stop. You're gonna kill him!"

But it was too late. He already had.

38

Ellie shoved the key into the lock and stumbled through her apartment door. Her shoulders drooped when she tossed her bag onto the floor by the coat rack and headed into the kitchen to deposit her gun in the safe over the refrigerator. The foul scent of bitter onions wafted to her nose as she lifted her arms. Sniffing her armpits, she grimaced.

It's been a hell of a week. I could use a good soak in the tub. And lots of soap.

The apartment was quiet. A single lamp beside the couch was lit. Next to the light, on the side table, sat a frame she'd never seen before. Ellie marveled at the image before picking it up, the brass rectangle heavy in her hand. A childlike drawing of a tall person with bright-red hair and a smaller person with blond braids rested beneath a layer of glass.

"Bet you can't guess who that is." Clay's hushed voice drifted over her shoulder.

Ellie turned to find him leaning against the wall of the hall, his thumbs hooked in the pockets of his Bermuda shorts and a huge grin fixed on his face. She mustered a smile for him. As exhausted as she was, the surprise was pleasant and worthy of praise. "Me and Beth."

He closed the gap and gave her a quick peck on the cheek. "She drew it this afternoon. We decided your living room needed a few pictures to liven the space up, so I went out and picked up a frame."

The memory of sitting in Melody Long's house snuck up on Ellie. She remembered the warmth she'd felt while staring at the pictures of smiling family members on the wall. And her jealousy at not having a similar warmth in her own home.

She traced a finger over the crayoned line of Bethany's face. Happiness warmed her cheeks. "I love it." She placed the frame back on the table.

Clay beamed and stuffed his hands into his pockets.

"It's quiet here." Ellie gazed down the hall.

"Jillian and Sam are spending the night at Jacob's."

"Where's Beth?" She touched her fingertip to the frame with Bethany's drawing.

I want to tell her how much I love this. How precious she is to me.

"Jillian made her a grilled cheese and got her ready for bed. I put Bethany to bed after she left. The kid conked out before I even finished reading this new Cinderella book your mom got for her." Clay ran a hand across the back of his head. "I never knew Cindy was so sassy."

Ellie chuckled. "Thanks. You've been waiting up for me since?"

"Yeah." He stepped behind Ellie and placed his hands on her shoulders, gently massaging her aching muscles. As he lowered his head next to hers, his lips tickled her earlobe. "But I don't mind waiting a little longer. Go take a hot shower and change into something more comfortable. I'll be here with a glass of wine when you get back."

He didn't have to tell her twice.

She turned and kissed him, long and soft. "Back in a minute."

On her way to a hot bath, she poked her head into Bethany's room. The little girl's long blond locks fanned out over her pillow. Her lips parted while she snored, and one of her arms hung over the side of her bed. Schneider lay below on the floor.

Ellie crept in and picked up the walrus. Bethany rolled as Ellie tucked the stuffed animal back into her arm. She brushed a strand of hair off her child's angelic face.

How is it possible to love this small human so much?

Bending down, Ellie placed a light kiss on the little girl's warm forehead. "I love the picture. Sweet dreams, Beth."

By the time Ellie trudged into her bathroom, she'd shed all her clothing across her bedroom floor. Steam rose from the tub as the water filled the bath. She undid her ponytail and brushed the tangles out of her hair, glancing at her reflection in a large mirror over the sink.

The rapidly rising heat brought a flush to her pale skin, but the dark shadows beneath her eyes remained. Her curls hung limp, like overcooked spaghetti, around her shoulders. She stopped brushing her hair and stared at the freckles sprinkled across her dull skin until the surface of the mirror fogged up.

Haggard. Drained. Hell, I look awful.

Ellie closed her eyes and inhaled the steamy air, expanding her lungs to the point where they threatened to burst. She held the breath, focusing her mind on the week's events. Monique's murder. Her mother's despair. Dan Jr.'s brush with death. Slowly, she opened her eyes and released the air from her lungs, along with the stress and tension in her soul.

She'd solved Monique's murder, her mother could start healing, and Dan Jr. was on the road to recovery.

No more problems to solve. Not at the moment, at least.

With careful movement, she rotated and sank into the bathtub. Hot water enveloped her tired limbs, soothing and cleansing them. Holding another breath, she dipped her head below the water, her hair floating on the surface.

There was no noise. No pain. Only her, suspended in silence, alone and in peace.

She stayed that way until bubbles escaped from the corners of her mouth.

Water rained off her as she sat upright, steamy air flooding her lungs. Fully relaxed, she reached for the loofah and bar of soap at the edge of the tub. She scraped the sponge against her body, expelling dry skin cells with each swipe.

Ellie finished her bath with a vigorous shampoo before slipping out and rinsing in the shower. She knew it was like double-dipping, but the thought of soaking in germs and dead skin cells turned her stomach.

On her bed, she'd set out a silk nightgown and robe. The smooth fabric engulfed her body like a soft cloud.

When she returned to the living room, she found Clay lounging on the couch, grasping the neck of an opened beer bottle and balancing the beverage on his thigh. True to his word, a freshly poured glass of wine waited for her on the coffee table.

He grinned as she approached. "So do you want to talk about your day or skip the replay?"

She sat beside him and reached for the wine glass. The aroma of blackberries made her smile as she sipped the sweet alcohol and contemplated the day's events. "I suppose you're pretty much up to speed on 'most everything already."

"Probably. The grapevine's been going nuts over what happened. I heard Chavin confessed."

Ellie placed her glass on the side table. "He did. You should've seen the hatred in his eyes. The pain. Kira Long's been running a grooming scheme for a decade now with those poor children at the LaPierre Foundation. I found a notebook in her apartment the day I went over to search for evidence. At the time, it just looked like random initials and numbers. I didn't realize I'd stumbled onto her bookkeeping."

"Are you sure Kira was the only one at LaPierre dipping her finger into the extra pie?" Clay raised the bottle to his lips and took a swig.

"I think a few of the foundation's lawyers were involved. We're still trying to determine how deep the corruption went." Ellie paused and retrieved her wine glass. She swirled the dark liquid inside the goblet. "If you're asking whether the LaPierres knew…Jackie says they didn't. I believe her… for now."

"What about…?" He hesitated.

"Kingsley?" Ellie finished for him. "I'll probably never know for sure, but I won't be surprised if that damned man didn't have his toe dipped into that swamp too."

"What do you think will happen?" Clay changed the subject away from the doctor who'd caused so much hell in Ellie's life. "To the LaPierre Foundation, I mean."

"Jackie told me she plans to step up and take the reins. With a much tighter grip than her parents held. I think she's done a lot of reflecting lately. About her adoption, and what her life could have been like if things had gone a different way. She could've been in Chavin's place. Her reflections changed the way she thought about her money and how to use her wealth and status."

Ellie's mind lingered on that statement. After the incident at the LaPierre mansion that afternoon, and a visit to the hospital to ensure Jackie didn't have a concussion, she'd driven her friend to a hotel for the night.

"Are you sure you should be alone?" Ellie eased her SUV past the iron gates of the mansion.

Jackie's head fell back against the headrest. "I won't be alone. I'll be in a building full of people."

"You know that's not what I meant." In less than a week, her friend lost her mother, an unborn sibling, and the man she loved. Ellie's heart ached for her.

"Everyone I care about is gone. There's not much I can do but be alone right now."

"You could stay at my place."

"No." Jackie swiveled to face Ellie. "I kind of want to be by myself for a while. There's a bunch of shit to sort out. With the foundation and with me. Despite what Greg claims, my parents intended for LaPierre to do good things, and only good things. It's a legacy I need...no, I want to carry on."

"So you're planning to take the reins?"

The corners of Jackie's mouth lifted into a ghost of a smile. "I am. Maybe start over from scratch, even. The LaPierre Foundation's name has been tainted. After the news hits the streets, any prestige the name carried will be gone. Besides, I always thought my family had a standoffish approach. No, I think I'll get a fresh team of people together, people I can trust. A new name. And we'll open centers closer to where help is needed."

Pride welled inside Ellie's chest. "Sounds like you've thought about this already."

"I have, actually. My parents' foundation always seemed to be about money to me. I want the nonprofit to have more purpose. Expand our offerings to more than money. Tutoring. Maybe art and music classes. Possibly daycare and vehicle programs in addition to job assistance. The things the community really needs. And not just for troubled kids. For all the kids with limited *opportunities. Perhaps if we show we care early on, fewer kids will end up like Greg."*

Ellie exhaled a heavy breath. "Restructuring the organization will take a lot of time and money."

Jackie stared at the roof of Ellie's SUV. "Good thing I've got plenty of both."

Ellie smiled. "Honestly? I think she may have finally found the calling she's been searching for all these years. She wants to do good with her family's fortune. And I think she'll succeed."

Clay took another swig of his beer, his Adam's apple bobbing in his neck. After finishing the drink, he smacked his lips and placed the empty bottle on the coffee table. "So do you believe what Chavin said?"

"Normally? Maybe not. The idea that children were being trafficked around the city to the Charleston elite for years and no one fought to free those kids? It's not something I want to believe, but…after everything both Bethany and I went through…" She shrugged.

If wishes were horses, beggars would ride.

She could almost hear her grandfather saying those exact words. Ellie didn't want to believe the world could be a horrible place, especially for children. But she did.

She pinched the fabric of her robe. The silk was smooth as butter as she rubbed the material between her fingertips. "But Kingsley had threads throughout the police departments. Especially the Charleston precinct. What if they're still there, Clay? Even though he's dead?"

He scratched his ear, pondering his answer. "With zombies, if you shoot the head, the body dies too. We can hope the same thing happened to Kingsley's network."

"Or maybe the network was already there. A different spider spun the original web. Kingsley was only the most recent arachnid to perch on it."

The idea soured the wine in Ellie's stomach. She returned her glass to the side table.

"The thought that a matrix of dirty cops is still in play at the precinct is horrifying," Clay bent forward and rested his elbows on his knees, "but not implausible. I've been hitting several roadblocks with my human-trafficking case. Even simple tasks are creating the biggest headaches for us. Makes me wonder how deep this corruption with Delecroix really goes."

"I'd guess pretty deep. This thing with LaPierre was sophisticated enough to stay under everyone's radar. Even Monique's. It was well-organized and probably backed by a ton of hush money to keep the people involved loyal. Like Kingsley's web that may or may not still be hanging around." Ellie flopped back against the couch and relaxed into the cushions.

Clay cleared his throat and locked eyes with her. "What about Lancaster? Do you think he killed Chavin on purpose to clean things up for someone?"

The steely glare in Lancaster's eyes as he fired the last shot into Greg Chavin's chest popped into Ellie's head. An icy chill slid down her spine. "The thought has crossed my mind a hundred times. We'll have to see what the officer-related shooting investigation says and then go from there." She took his hand. "We need to find out the truth."

"Do you need something to take your mind off things?"

Clay leaned over and laid his hand on Ellie's thigh. His lips hovered inches away from hers.

Beneath her nightgown, her flesh tingled at his touch. She stroked the curve of his chin. Her heartbeat quickened as his hand roamed higher, trailing his nail along the barrier separating silk from skin. She roped her arms around his neck and grinned.

"Please. That's a problem for another day."

39

Sunlight glared down from the clear blue sky as Ellie bent and slipped a backpack strap over Bethany's arm. A bell rang, the chime slicing through the hustle and bustle happening amid the crowd of parents and students on the school's front lawn.

"You have the card you made and the gift for your friend?"

"Right here." Bethany reached around and patted the protruding pocket on the side of her backpack. Strands of her blond hair practically glittered in the bright rays.

Ellie kissed the top of her head. "All right, have a good day. I'll pick you up this afternoon. Maybe we can run out for ice cream? Now that I've finished my case, I'm hoping we'll get to spend more time together this week."

"I'd like that." Bethany's head dipped toward the sidewalk. She dragged the toe of her tennis shoe over a crack in the cement. "I missed you last week. Maybe we can do something special for dinner tonight? With just you and me? And Schneider? We can talk about things."

"That sounds perfect. Any things in particular?"

Bethany shrugged. "I dunno. Whatever we feel like, I guess." She waved at Ellie and skipped off toward the school entrance.

Ellie's lips curled into a smile as she walked back to her SUV. Finally, she and Beth would get some quality time together. After the craziness of the previous week, she ached for downtime with her foster daughter. And maybe she could start looking for a new house with a yard big enough for a little girl to play in.

And a puppy too.

Her phone buzzed when she rounded the back of her vehicle. Ellie retrieved the device from her pocket and glanced at the caller ID. Her stomach tightened.

Stoddard's name flashed across the screen.

What if I didn't answer?

She'd earned a day or two off, hadn't she? Even her brother's hospitalization hadn't kept her from working her case. A case she closed. Her thumb hovered over the *accept* and *decline* options.

A butterfly landed on the SUV's back window and studied her.

Ellie leaned in to appreciate the orange-and-yellow pattern on the insect's wings. "What's it like? To be free?" The butterfly refused to answer, instead flittering off on the tail end of the breeze into a patch of tiny purple flowers.

With a sigh, she pressed her thumb on the screen and held the phone to her ear.

"Detective Kline. Were you busy?" Stoddard's words came out in a rush. "Good job on the LaPierre case. Our higher-ups are pleased."

The praise ruffled Ellie's feathers. "Pleased that the killer was found, or pleased that the killer was a lower-class nobody and not one of the Charleston elite?"

Stoddard paused. "On record? The first one. Off? Both."

The answer did little to ease Ellie's fears. Greg Chavin had mentioned missing kids, and she knew of two case files involving missing LaPierre recipients that were shoved into a box and left to collect dust on a shelf in the cold case room. The bare minimum of investigation had been conducted to find them. Was that by the higher-ups' command? Had the Charleston Police Department aided Kira and her associates in their human trafficking ring?

Goose bumps scrambled up Ellie's arms. If so, the web of corruption still lingered in the precinct. The first chance she got, she intended to check the log-in sheet for those boxes and find out who handled the case.

"There's no rest for the wicked, though." Stoddard clicked her tongue. "We've got a body in the Charleston Financial District. I need you there. Now."

The back of Ellie's neck tightened. "Why me? I just closed a big case. Don't I get time to decompress?"

"Because your skill set puts you in a unique position to assist." The nonchalant tone in Stoddard's voice grated on her nerves.

"By skill set, you mean my social status." Ellie rubbed her temple.

I promised Beth we'd spend more time together. I can't go back on my word. Not again.

Time was precious to Ellie. Her brother's brush with death had shown her how things could change at a moment's notice. She didn't want to spend all her remaining time chasing leads and risking her life.

Bethany missed her. Clay missed her. They were her family, and she intended to give them the attention they deserved with whatever time she had left.

A tapping erupted on the other end of the line, like Stoddard was rapping a pencil tip against the desk. "Detective Kline? You still there?"

The work-life balance was still a work-in-progress for Ellie. She hadn't yet found her footing, but she'd keep trying. For Clay and Bethany.

There's a way I can be a good detective, a good mom, and a good girlfriend. Better time management. Reorganization of my priorities. I can make this work. I know I can.

For now, work was top of the priority list. At least, until she needed to pick Bethany up from school. She'd promised her ice cream and a family dinner, a date she was determined to keep.

Ellie walked around her SUV and opened the door. "What's going on?" She started the ignition and flipped the air conditioning on full blast.

"The victim was a bodyguard assigned to protect a local state senator. We have reason to believe the senator may be the killer's next target." Stoddard cleared her throat with a high-pitched *hrrmm* that scraped against Ellie's eardrum. "Obviously, this highly sensitive case needs to be resolved as soon as possible."

Another case with ties to high society. Ellie pictured Greg Chavin lying on the blue, marbled stone floor of Jackie's kitchen. The way his glassy eyes gazed at her as the light behind them died. The way the blood staining his shirt formed a shape similar to a Rorschach test pattern.

"Poor people like me...the have-nots...don't get law and order..."

Monique LaPierre got justice for her murder. She was a have. Greg Chavin was denied justice and continually victimized. He was a have-not. Ellie's gut twisted into a knot.

"Detective Kline? Are you still there?" The tapping on Stoddard's end of the line intensified.

Ellie pressed a button on the driver's side door. The windows, cracked to keep the vehicle from turning into a kiln, rolled shut. She peered through the windshield at the city beyond the school.

Down the road, a flock of birds dove from a white church steeple and soared into the clear sky. Across the street, a couple chatted as they exited a gym carrying yoga totes and water bottles. Above them, a paunchy man on a tall ladder washed windows.

Her attention fell on two scruffy teenagers riding on the same bike, one of them with his arms wrapped tight around the other's waist, laughing and racing down the street. An old woman walking a fluffy dog on the sidewalk stopped to shake her head at the youthful antics.

Ellie had signed up to protect the people of Charleston. All the people, both the poor and the rich. The old and the young. The good and the bad. Justice was justice, no matter the tax bracket or race or generation the victim belonged to.

She placed her hand on the steering wheel.

"Text me the address. I'm on my way."

The End
To be continued...

Thank you for reading.
All of the *Ellie Kline* series books can be found on Amazon.

ACKNOWLEDGMENTS

How does one adequately express gratitude to all those who have transformed a shared dream into a stunning reality? Let us attempt to do just that.

First and foremost, our families deserve our deepest thanks. Their unwavering support and encouragement have been our bedrock, allowing us the time and energy to translate our collective imagination into the words that fill these pages. Their belief in our vision has been a constant source of strength and inspiration.

As coauthors, our journey has been uniquely collaborative and rewarding. Now, with Mary also embracing the additional role of publisher, our adventure has taken on an exciting new dimension. This transition from solely writing to also publishing has been both a challenge and a joy, opening doors to share our work more directly with you, our readers.

We are immensely grateful to the entire team at Mary Stone Publishing — a group who believed in our potential from the very beginning. Their commitment extends beyond editing our words; it encompasses the tireless efforts of designers, marketers, and support staff, all dedicated to bringing our stories to life. Their expertise, creativity, and passion have been vital in capturing the essence of our tales and sharing them with the world.

However, our greatest appreciation is reserved for you, our beloved readers. You took a chance on our book, generously sharing your most precious asset—your time. It is our fervent hope that the pages of this book have rewarded that generosity, offering you a journey worth taking and memories that linger.

With all our love and heartfelt appreciation,

Mary & Donna

ABOUT THE AUTHOR

Nestled in the serene Blue Ridge Mountains of East Tennessee, Mary Stone crafts her stories surrounded by the natural beauty that inspires her. What was once a home filled with the lively energy of her sons has now become a peaceful writer's retreat, shared with cherished pets and the vivid characters of her imagination.

As her sons grew and welcomed wonderful daughters-in-law into the family, Mary's life entered a quieter phase, rich with opportunities for deep creative focus. In this tranquil environment, she weaves tales of courage, resilience, and intrigue, each story a testament to her evolving journey as a writer.

From childhood fears of shadowy figures under the bed to a profound understanding of humanity's real-life villains, Mary's style has been shaped by the realization that the most complex antagonists often hide in plain sight. Her writing is characterized by strong, multifaceted heroines who defy traditional roles, standing as equals among their peers in a world of suspense and danger.

Mary's career has blossomed from being a solitary author to establishing her own publishing house—a significant milestone that marks her growth in the literary world. This expansion is not just a personal achievement but a reflection of her commitment to bring thrilling and thought-provoking stories to a wider audience. As an author and publisher, Mary continues to challenge the conventions of the thriller genre, inviting readers into gripping tales filled with serial killers, astute FBI agents, and intrepid heroines who confront peril with unflinching bravery.

Each new story from Mary's pen—or her publishing house—is a pledge to captivate, thrill, and inspire, continuing the legacy of the imaginative little girl who once found wonder and mystery in the shadows.

Discover more about Mary Stone on her website.
www.authormarystone.com

Donna Berdel

Raised as an Army brat, Donna has lived all over the world, but no place has given her as much peace as the home she lives in with her husband near Myrtle Beach. But while she now keeps her feet planted firmly in the sand, her mind goes back to those cities and the people she met and said goodbye to so many times.

With her two adopted cats fighting for lap space, she brings those she loved (and those she didn't) back as characters in her books. And yes, it's kind of fun to kill off anyone who was mean to her in the past. Mean clerk at the grocery store...beware!

Connect with Mary online

- facebook.com/authormarystone
- x.com/MaryStoneAuthor
- goodreads.com/AuthorMaryStone
- bookbub.com/profile/3378576590
- pinterest.com/MaryStoneAuthor
- instagram.com/marystoneauthor
- tiktok.com/@authormarystone

Printed in Great Britain
by Amazon